"You will move into a room near mine tonight!"

Christian's flat announcement made Emily jerk her head around in alarm. "Whatever for?"

"For your safety, Emily."

"Oh!" Thrown into confusion, she searched her shattered thoughts. "You think Greg Vernon might come creeping back to finish what he tried to start?"

"It is possible!" Christian's voice was as hard as steel.

Having abandoned her intended career for marriage, *ROSALIE ASH* spent several years as a bilingual personal assistant to the managing director of a leisure group. She now lives in Warwickshire with her husband and her daughters, Kate and Abby, and her lifelong enjoyment of writing has led to her career as a novelist. Her interests include languages, travel and research for her books, reading and visits to the Royal Shakespeare Theatre in nearby Stratford-upon-Avon. Other pleasures include swimming, yoga and country walks.

ROSALIE ASH

Original Sin

Harlequin Books

TORONTO • NEW YORK • LONDON
AMSTERDAM • PARIS • SYDNEY • HAMBURG
STOCKHOLM • ATHENS • TOKYO • MILAN
MADRID • WARSAW • BUDAPEST • AUCKLAND

ISBN 0-373-11723-X

ORIGINAL SIN

Copyright © 1993 by Rosalie Ash.

First North American Publication 1995.

Printed in U.S.A.

CHAPTER ONE

AT THE sound of the spit of gravel on the drive below, Emily jumped out of the bath, short strawberry-blonde curls still damp from a hasty hairwash, and went to peer curiously from the open window of her bedroom.

The warm July air met her, redolent with the rich, sweet scent of golden broom, pine trees and some other heady, elusive fragrance, some musky blend of smells unique to summers in France. A distant flash of black wings circled in the evening sky around the mossy red pantiled roof and tall chimneys of the opposite wing of the château. Bats, probably, Emily decided, thinking how neatly this ancient creeper-clad building lent itself to the occupation of bats in its belfry...

Clutching the ends of the big ivory bath-towel around herself, she shrank back behind the heavy curtain to see a sleek open-top Mercedes sports car sweeping into the courtyard, to halt outside the entrance to the château.

It wasn't really dark yet. Just dusk. The arc of yellow light from the storm light below showed a tall, broad-shouldered man springing athletically from the driver's seat. Snatching a battered-looking briefcase or flight-bag from inside the car, he thrust his fingers through the lock of dark hair which fell over his forehead and headed, with a purposeful yet oddly preoccupied air, towards the steps. There was a loping spring in his movements which reminded Emily of a lion's prowl...

Could this be her new boss? Instinct told her it was, even though Lisette Duvert, taken by surprise this morning at Emily's arrival a day earlier than expected, had predicted that Monsieur Malraux wouldn't be getting back from his business trip until tomorrow. The new arrival had a distinctly boss-like air about him, Emily told herself, suppressing a smile. He looked as if he exuded that god-like air of indispensability. As if the universe would have quite a struggle continuing to function without him...

She'd better get dried, dressed, and somehow find her way down to announce her presence. Lisette Duvert, the young, glamorous and rather unhelpful housekeeper, had shown her to her room, announced that tonight was her night off, and promptly departed. Emily had been left with vague directions to the nearest restaurant for an evening meal, and with the uncomfortable feeling that she might be the only member of staff of the Château de Mordin spending the night here. She wasn't normally prey to nervous fantasy, but she'd seriously considered jumping back in her hired Renault 5 and driving into Saintes, to see if her old penfriend Marianne and family would put her up for the night...

Before she could make any move towards drying and dressing, however, heavy footsteps sounded on the landing outside her door, and without warning the door was pushed open. A man around her own age, of average height and solid build, with curly brown hair, definitely not the recent arrival from the Mercedes, marched into the room, swung a rucksack on to the bed, and began to discard a short-sleeved red shirt as he strode towards the bathroom.

'Hey...!' Her indignant gasp brought the intruder to an abrupt halt, and with a muffled exclamation he reached to switch on the light, then gazed with an unrepentant leer at the sight of Emily, clutching her towel round her slender body, pale with outrage.

'Well, well! *Definitely* all mod cons!' The voice was English, with a slight regional accent. Hazel eyes gleamed with undisguised appreciation. 'French, English or German?'

'Whoever you are, will you please get out of my room?'

'Ah, English. Lisette didn't tell me I was sharing, but I've no objections if you haven't. Greg Vernon's the name. I'm hitching round Europe, doing a spot of casual summer work when I can. And you?'

Emily glared at the man, longing for some object to throw.

'Emily Gainsborough. I'm here to do temporary work for the summer, too. And I'm delighted to meet you, but perhaps we could continue this friendly chat some other time? This is *my* room!'

Greg Vernon's eyes were overtly curious as he examined her long, slim legs, the petite line of her hips and breasts covered by the towel, the delicate swell of her breasts above, and the damp, feathery gold curls clinging to her head.

'Lisette told me third door on the right.'

'Maybe counting's not your strong point?' she suggested cuttingly.

'So what are you supposed to be doing here? Odd jobs, like me?' Greg Vernon ignored her sarcasm, folding his arms and staring hard at the curve of her thighs.

Humouring the man seemed the only option for the moment. She tightened her hold on the towel, and controlled her temper.

'No, I'm a temporary secretary for the château owner. Until I take up a full-time job in the Foreign Office in September. Now would you please . . . ?'

'The Foreign Office?'

'Yes. At their Paris embassy.' Alone in this apparently deserted château, Emily was feeling acutely vulnerable. Even if she knew she could probably look after herself, it didn't dispel her sense of female vulnerability. She didn't like the way he was ogling her. If she leaned out of the window and screamed, would someone come to her aid?

'Brainy as well as beautiful?' He sounded impressed. 'How old are you, sweetheart?'

'I'm not your sweetheart. And I'm old enough to look after myself. Now will you please go and find yourself an *empty* room?'

'You're a sight for very sore eyes, did you know that?' he persisted, his grin widening. 'I've got a soft spot for brainy brown-eyed strawberry blondes.'

'Will you just get out of here?'

'Especially brown-eyed strawberry blondes with cheekbones like Kim Basinger's, who look as if a gust of wind would blow them over,' he mused, unaffected by the glitter of fury in her eyes. He took a few steps towards her on sturdy, muscular legs with just a hint of bravado swagger. 'What do you say to giving my back a scrub in the bath, sweetheart? I'll make it worth your while...'

'I'm warning you,' she hissed in a low, shaky voice. 'If you don't get out of my room in five seconds flat, I'll...'

'You'll what, sweetheart?'

The masculine goad, the insultingly confident hand reaching towards her, was the deciding factor. Fear abruptly left her. Calmly, with a re-action born of weekly practice at her local sports centre, and several competition wins at national level, she caught his upper arm in a classic judo hold. Before he knew what had hit him, Greg Vernon flipped over to land flat on his back on the floor on the landing outside Emily's room.

Winded, he lay there, staring up at her. The look of stunned surprise on his face was so comical, she had to fight back shaky laughter as she slammed the door on him.

The towel, loosened in the struggle, suddenly fell to the floor. For a few unavoidable seconds, Emily found herself stark naked, trembling all over, slender thighs braced, small, high, ochre-tipped breasts rising and falling rapidly, and she was just about to snatch her salmon-pink satin wrap from the bed when another voice spoke from the reopened doorway. A deep, scathing, sardonic voice which made her jerk round in dismay.

'Mademoiselle Gainsborough?'

Beneath an unruly lock of straight black hair, intense, black-fringed smoke-blue eyes met Emily's wide, slanting brown ones. A rush of heat prickled all over her body as she stared up at the tall, dark man. It was the Mercedes owner, in slate-grey suit, white silk shirt and discreetly patterned silk tie, absorbing the scene, and her nakedness, with a totally deadpan expression. A jagged scar ran down his left cheek. Harsh lines of cynicism and bitterness were scored around his mouth. And yet somehow he was still the most devastatingly attractive man she'd ever seen.

It was only a split second between his appearance and her physical reaction to cover herself up, but it seemed extraordinarily prolonged, as if time had suddenly switched into slow motion.

Opening her mouth to speak, she found that no words would emerge. She settled for a quick nod, and dived, utterly mortified, for the wrap, plunging her arms in and clutching it round herself with trembling fingers. She was going hot and cold alternately; groaning inwardly. The incident with Greg Vernon had been bad enough. To be facing her new employer, in the nude and with a strange male flat-out on the landing floor...*not* the most auspicious of starts...

'Would you mind explaining what is going on here?'

'This man barged into my room, and tried to...to molest me. I'm afraid I used self-defence automatically...'

'So I had the pleasure of witnessing just now. It is strange, *mademoiselle*, but I don't recall any mention of naked martial arts on your curriculum vitae.'

His English accent was near perfect, with a slight American twang, as if he'd learned it in the States rather than in England. There was a glitter of some emotion in his eyes. Emily thought she detected the faintest suggestion of humour, then decided she'd been mistaken. He definitely looked *unamused*.

Greg Vernon was dragging himself to his feet, ruefully rubbing his hipbone.

'She's lethal. Sorry mate.' He sounded shaken, though slightly sullen. He made a lunge for his rucksack and looked anxious to leave. 'Are you the new owner of this place?'

The dark man nodded curtly. 'Christian Malraux. And, according to my housekeeper's note, I assume that you must be Greg Vernon?'

'The same. Wrong room. Bit of a mix-up...'

'Get out, right now.' The ice in the deep voice sent chills down Emily's spine. She'd been right. He was *not* amused.

'Now, wait a minute...'

'Out. You're sacked.' There was no emotion, no trace of uncertainty. Just harsh, judgemental finality.

'Sacked? I haven't even started yet. But you can stick your flaming job right up your...'

With a lightning reflex, the tall, athletic-looking Frenchman had levered himself away from the doorjamb and taken the other man by one arm, jerking it expertly up his back, immobilising him.

'Guard your tongue,' he ordered softly, 'and get off my property.'

With a warning thrust, he released him again. Greg Vernon's shoulders and back bunched in anger, but he clearly thought better of further challenge. There was an indefinable air of toughness about Christian Malraux; the jagged scar lent a slightly sinister air to his appearance. He stood back to let Greg Vernon through, and Emily, for some perverse reason she hardly understood, felt compelled to speak up on his behalf.

'There's no need to fire him on my account,' she protested quickly, hugging the satin wrap closely around her as the smoky-blue eyes turned their chill intensity on her again.

'Indeed?' The deep voice was taunting. Transfixed, she stared at the dark face, frantically trying to analyse why he should be so unsettling. Taken separately, his features were strong, but otherwise unremarkable. He had a large nose, deep-set, deceptively sleepy blue eyes, a wide, hard mouth and a jutting chin with a cleft in the centre. A bluish black shadow on his lower jaw proclaimed his need to shave at least twice a day.

'Is this man a friend of yours, mademoiselle?'

'No. But I think it was just a silly...misunderstanding. I think Mr Vernon and I understand each other now.'

'I am sure that you do.' The harsh, husky timbre of his voice brought goose-bumps out all over her skin. 'However, I make the decisions here. I will see you downstairs in ten minutes, Mademoiselle Gainsborough. Keep your door locked in future. Particularly when you are taking a bath.'

With a final penetrating appraisal of her appearance, leaving her feeling stripped naked all over again, he withdrew from the room and shut the door with a decisive click.

Emily leaned against the closed door, and shut her eyes. Arrogant, supercilious man, she muttered out loud. She was shaking, so violently that she could hardly turn the key in the lock.

Why was she so angry with Christian Malraux? she wondered, as she went through automatic motions of dressing, her thoughts flitting wildly. Surely she should be angry with the Englishman? Glad of her employer's timely intervention? Instead she found herself feeling almost sorry for her brash would-be attacker, and furiously resentful of the patronising, judgemental attitude of Christian Malraux...

Dragging a hairbrush through her short sunset-gold curls, she glared at her reflection. Demure now in knee-length salmon silk sarong-skirt, chocolate silk camisole and loose salmon silk collarless overshirt, she carefully fitted delicate pearl-drop earrings, and slicked a touch of pale pink lipstick over her lips, and gold-brown shadow on her lids. The look was cool, casually elegant, smart enough to cope with any eventuality. Dressed this way she might, just, be able to retrieve her credibility and poise.

As she made her way reluctantly down to meet her new employer, she came to a rueful conclusion about her muddled feelings. She'd managed to get the better of Greg Vernon. She had his measure. She'd met men like him before, and handled them with relative ease. Somehow he presented no threat. Not so with Christian Malraux. She had the feeling he was the kind of man it would be very hard to get the better of. And he seemed to present the biggest threat of all...

'Have you eaten?' the question was barked without preamble. She blinked at him in surprise.

'No...'

'*Bon. Ça c'est la première chose à faire*...first, we eat.'

No consultation. No prevarication. Christian Malraux was cool, calm, and in a disinterested sort of way totally in control. She found herself escorted firmly to the gunmetal-grey Mercedes, and then speeding back down the long, shingled drive of the château towards the stone gateway. The headlights lit up massive cedar trees, walnut trees, arcing through the dense parkland. A rabbit froze in the brilliant beam for a split second, then bounded desperately away into the undergrowth.

'So you arrived early,' he said expressionlessly. 'Lisette was not expecting you until tomorrow.'

'There must have been a misunderstanding. I was under the impression I was due to start today.'

The shadowed face flicked briefly towards her, then fixed ahead in concentration on driving expertly fast along the winding country roads.

'Lisette also thought you weren't due back from your business trip until tomorrow!' she added calmly, marvelling how composed she could sound when inside she was a quivering jelly of nerves and reaction. Sitting here in the open Mercedes, beside Christian Malraux, she was experiencing the most unnerving *déjà vu* sensation, as if she'd driven with him before, had known him before, as if he was someone important in her life, someone with a deep connection on another, subconscious level.

Since his saturnine appearance at her bedroom door, he'd swapped the grey suit for stone-coloured fine gabardine trousers, a black cotton mesh collarless shirt, and a loose, unstructured stone cotton jacket. He looked expensively casual, European designer-style. And heart-stoppingly attractive. Privately she decided Christian Malraux could probably manage to dress in a frilly pink sundress and still set every female heart within a two-mile radius thudding in ecstasy.

'My meetings finished earlier than expected,' he informed her harshly. 'Which, from what I saw tonight, is just as well.'

'If you're referring to Greg Vernon, I was quite capable of dealing with him myself!'

'So I saw. But I suspect you had an element of luck on your side, Mademoiselle Gainsborough. Never underestimate your adversary. Once that initial element of surprise is gone, you would do well to remember that.'

'I happen to possess a brown belt in judo,' she told him with calm pride. 'A friend's father is an instructor. I've fought in national competitions.'

'Impressive.' He didn't sound particularly impressed. The dark face turned briefly in her direction again, and she sensed a mocking smile. 'I know something of the martial arts myself. Your performance was certainly entertaining. But your linguistic and secretarial qualifications will be of more use to me.'

'Oh, I'm definitely versatile!'

His glance was sardonic. Instantly she wished she hadn't bothered with the flippant response. Her face was burning again in the darkness as she briefly relived the scene in her bedroom. She sought quickly to change the subject on to something less personal.

'Did I get the impression you'd recently taken over the château, Monsieur Malraux?'

'Three months ago.' He nodded in the darkness. They were approaching some lights on the left now, pulling off the road beside a restaurant which looked as if it had been converted from an old mill.

'You bought it from the previous owner?'

He shook his head briefly. 'Years ago I lived at the château, with my uncle and aunt. But I chose another career, which took me abroad. I had not been back to Château de Mordin for five years. Until my uncle was taken ill and then died.'

Emily had the strong impression that Christian Malraux was far from delighted to be back at the château now. There was a cool cynicism underlying his words.

The cynicism she found hard to relate to. Casting embarrassment aside, her own emotions felt heightened. She found it hard to explain how she was feeling, even to herself. All she knew was that from the moment he'd appeared in her bedroom doorway she'd felt as if some obscure inner organ of her body had gone into slow meltdown. Combined with embarrassment at the scene he'd interrupted, and resentment at his authoritarian manner, this was a bewildering reaction. She was feeling slightly breathless, and shivery, and decidedly dithery...

With such a sharp focus on her own emotions it simply wasn't fair to sense that Christian Malraux was offhandedly doing his duty, escorting his new secretary out for a meal on her first night, with his thoughts and his heart far away on some other, more enthralling life he'd been forced to abandon...

She caught herself up sharply. What idiotic fantasies were these? How could she be allowing

her brain to run riot with such adolescent melo-
drama? She was twenty-two, a languages
graduate filling in the summer before taking up
a responsible job at an embassy. To date she'd
had countless casual boyfriends—enjoyed lots of
platonic friendships with the opposite sex, too.
How could she be feeling this...this illogical
kaleidoscope of emotion half an hour after
meeting Christian Malraux?

She resolved to take a stern grip on herself.

But inside the restaurant, seated opposite her
new employer at a check-clothed table, she met
the smoky, sleepy, slightly bored blue gaze across
the menu and felt the breath knocked out of her
lungs again.

'Seafood of all kinds is excellent in Charente
Maritime,' he told her coolly, assessing the slight
involuntary flush of her cheeks with an air of
detachment. 'Just about every kind of fish that
swims in the sea is caught and cooked and coated
in some cunning sauce.'

'Yes...I already know the area. That's the
main reason I chose this particular job. I have a
penfriend fairly close by. I used to spend summers
with her and her family.'

'Where do they live?' The query was
perfunctory.

'Saintes.'

'A beautiful town. The Roman amphitheatre
is extraordinary.'

'Yes...' She studied the menu unseeingly. This
cool small talk was somehow infinitely disturbing. 'I...I think I'll have the *raie*.'

'Would you like some wine?'

She nodded. 'Château de Mordin produce a Sauvignon, don't they?'

A slow smile altered the brooding darkness of the face opposite her. He thrust long, spatulate fingers through the persistent fall of dark hair on his forehead, and narrowed his blue eyes speculatively.

'You have already done your homework, *mademoiselle*?'

'I'm a naturally inquisitive person. Château de Mordin houses a co-operative of a hundred and forty-five vine growers, covering seven hundred hectares. You primarily make *pineau cognac*, which is one part cognac to three parts grape juice, with wines a secondary product. You produce three white wines, including a *cuvée speciale*, plus a *rosé* and a red.'

He laughed, completely demolishing her fragile composure. Christian Malraux had a deep, husky, infectious laugh and excellent, even white teeth. The slash of brilliance against the dusky tan of his skin make her think, irrationally, of pirates.

'Little Miss Efficiency. My friend at your college was right when he said I'd be sorry to lose you.'

Emily was appalled to find herself blushing. Even more mortified when she realised that Christian Malraux was aware of her hot cheeks.

'What an intriguing mixture you are, *mademoiselle* ...'

'Please, call me Emily!' she snapped, pressing her hands together in the soft silk of her lap, willing herself to be cool and collected.

'Emily.' He said it consideringly, rolling the syllables deliberately, teasing around his tongue, his accent more in evidence. *'Oui, d'accord.* Emily. You must call me Christian.'

There was a momentary pause. Lost in the sleepy black-fringed blue eyes, Emily found she was holding her breath.

'Yes. Thank you...Christian.' She'd only spoken the man's first name, for heaven's sake. She felt as tense as if she'd just confessed some intimate secret...

The waiter came. Christian dispatched their order, then turned his attention back to her still-flushed face.

'As I was saying,' he continued softly, as if there'd been no interruption, 'you are an intriguing mixture, Emily. Cool enough to use judo successfully against a man, to defend yourself. Professional enough to carry out detailed background research for what is merely a temporary job. Yet you look so fragile, as if a man could crush you if he held you too tightly.'

'I...'

'And shy enough to blush like a schoolgirl when you are paid a compliment.'

'I don't normally blush!' she protested with a soft vehemence which clearly amused him even more. 'You'll have to excuse me. I'm feeling a little...off balance tonight. For obvious reasons!'

'Ah. You mean your enchanting...nudity...on our first meeting?' he goaded, equally soft. The smile sent her into a helpless inner tailspin. 'Or perhaps you mean you are still shaken by the unpleasant incident with Vernon?'

'Both,' she agreed shortly, glancing up in some relief as their wine arrived. 'You know, I came here this summer to brush up my business French,' she went on hurriedly, desperate to switch the persistent spotlight off herself and her emotions, 'yet we've done nothing but speak English.'

'We are not talking business, Emily.' Wretched man. He was enjoying watching her squirm!

'No...'

'Shall we agree to speak French in the vineyard office?'

'I suppose so.'

He was humouring her, she recognised frustratedly. Her new employer was obviously finding her intensely amusing. She took a long mouthful of the cool white wine. It tasted faintly of apricots and wild herbs, with a crisp refreshing bite to it. A basket of aromatic fresh bread had been placed on the table. She realised how hungry she was. Tension or no tension, with or without Christian Malraux's extremely unchivalrous taunts, she was going to enjoy this meal.

To distract herself from the mocking blue eyes she inspected her surroundings in greater detail. The restaurant was busy, buzzing with talk and laughter. Several French families were eating, plus a sprinkling of Germans, and English. Behind her she could hear voices in her native tongue busily deciphering the intricacies of the fish menu with the aid of a dictionary.

'This is an attractive restaurant,' she murmured politely, switching into French deliberately. 'Is there still a mill-wheel?'

'Yes. If we'd wanted to we could have sat outside on the grass, near the mill-stream,' Christian confirmed coolly, also switching to French. 'But the mosquitoes can be unpleasant.'

'Another time I'll wear repellent. I love eating out of doors. It's such a luxury in England.'

'Tomorrow night I will bring you here, and you may cover yourself in insect repellent and sit by the mill-stream, Emily.'

'Oh, I wasn't suggesting that you bring me here again...'

'Do not begin blushing again,' he advised her, with a lazy, speculative grin.

'I wasn't!'

But she felt on fire all over as his casual gaze moved slowly, assessingly, from the top of her copper-blonde head, down over her wide brown eyes to the petite curves of her breasts under the silk camisole. Braless, she felt, to her acute chagrin, the tips of her breasts begin to tighten involuntarily in response to that challenging appraisal.

'Your French is excellent, Emily,' he praised quietly, leaning nonchalently back in his chair and sliding his hands into his jacket pockets. 'Is your Spanish also as good?'

'Reasonable. I suspect my French is better, because I've spent more time in France. With my penfriend's family. In my teens. So...' she sought, once again, to switch the subject, to shrink back from the spotlight '...what was the career which took you abroad so much?'

'Journalism.'

Did she imagine the slight hardening of the lines around Christian's mouth? The slight withdrawal?

'What sort of journalism?'

'I was a foreign correspondent on a national newspaper. Then I reported foreign news for television.'

'I see.' She stared at him in mounting curiosity. Their first course had arrived, a platter of fresh *langoustines*, and she picked thoughtfully at one of the rigid shells with her fingers, finding herself staring at the beady little eyes of the shellfish with an abrupt shudder of sympathy.

Was this why Christian Malraux had an air of embittered cynicism? Foreign news reporting was an unremitting diet of wars, famine and atrocities, wasn't it?

'Did you throw it all in because your uncle was taken ill?'

'Not entirely. I'd been contemplating making a change, finding a way to get back down to earth, literally as well as metaphorically. TV news reporting can become dangerously addictive. All the flying bullets and front-line bulletins...'

She found herself staring at the scar on his cheek, imagining some hair-raising incident with

guerrillas and machine guns. She winced involuntarily, and he saw her reaction, touching the
scar with a grim smile.

'This disfigurement has no connection with my
TV journalism. But does it disgust you, Emily?'
He sounded bleakly amused.

'*No!*' She shook her head with some force.
'No, it most certainly does not disgust me! What
a ridiculous suggestion!'

Christian's gaze had narrowed at her ve-
hement denial. There was a brief silence, then he
shrugged, with a slight smile.

'You do not need to burst with righteous in-
dignation, Emily. I believe you.'

A longer pause stretched out between them,
and then with thoughtful deliberation Christian
reached across the table, and took her left hand
in his, lightly, turning it over to inspect the narrow
palm, the long, slim, ringless fingers.

The clasp was impersonal, exploratory. His
skin felt warm and dry, his fingers lean and
powerful, as if his strength was a latent threat,
held in careful reserve.

Emily could hardly breathe. She felt as if
something was constricting her windpipe. She
stared down at their joined hands, at the strong,
dark, hair-roughened back of Christian's right
hand encompassing hers. How could something
as simple and innocent as a touching of hands
feel so intensely intimate...so annihilating to her
senses?

Her heart was thudding painfully hard against
her breastbone. She tried to shrug off this over-

whelming emotion, this warm, shimmering sensation mysteriously forcing up her blood-pressure, speeding up her pulse-rate, but failed spectacularly.

'No rings?' Christian sounded dismissive, releasing her hand with a composure she yearned to emulate.

'No...' Resisting the urge to snatch her hand defensively into her lap, she transferred it slowly to her wine glass, proud of her precision control. She took a careful sip of wine.

'No ties, no commitments?' He persisted coolly.

'None. That's the way I intend things to stay.'

'Hence the high-powered Foreign Office job in September?'

She nodded, warming to her impressive display of indifference. Her stomach was in knots. Her heart was racing at twice its normal speed.

'Too many of my friends finished higher education only to throw it all away to get married! I have a very clear-cut vision of where I'm heading for, and its *not* the altar!'

Even as she heard herself say it, she was mentally floundering in a warm dark whirlpool of reaction to his touch, his voice, everything about him...

'Wise girl,' he approved softly. 'Stick to your career. Don't be side-tracked. Love is a destructive emotion.'

With a smiling nod, she stared at him in silence. Her throat felt curiously tight. He'd caught her on the raw again. As if he'd aimed a sharp punch to her solar plexus.

Their food arrived, a welcome diversion. She tackled the delicious skate in caper sauce, absently sliding the white fish off the smooth webbed bone with her fork.

'Love is a *destructive* emotion? That's going a bit far, surely?' she teased lightly, glancing up when she felt sure she had her emotions under tight control. 'You sound deeply embittered!'

Christian had opted for a rare *filet mignon*, oozing pink juices and exuding a rich, savoury aroma. He was eating it with the kind of uninhibited relish Emily decided might be a national characteristic.

'Life has taught me the value of independence. Take my advice: keep your heart to yourself, Emily.'

The flat words were unemotional. She felt herself go very still, staring warily into the deep-set gaze.

Abruptly, totally without warning, she felt as if she'd stumbled into an entirely new landscape of emotions. In a moment maybe she'd wake up and find she was sleepwalking...

This was awful. This was unthinkable. First the unfortunate introduction, now some sort of humiliating mind-reading. Had he taken a subtle glance inside her head, read her splintering composure, identified it for what it seemed to be? Her very first, long-retarded, breathless, hopeless 'crush', overwhelming her as irrepressibly as a bout of flu? What would her brother Ben make of her behaviour tonight? she wondered distractedly. Would he believe his eyes if he saw his brainy little sister, cool and pragmatic, independent and resourceful, tumbling into a crazy, mindless infatuation with a man she'd met barely an hour and a half before?

CHAPTER TWO

ABRUPTLY Emily pushed her knife and fork together.

'Lost your appetite?' The deep voice was expressionless.

'Sort of.'

'Would you like dessert? Coffee?'

'Nothing else. I'm feeling sleepy. Travelling affects me like that.'

'Then I had better take you back to bed, Emily.'

His words hung between them, like a teasing challenge. Had he intended any double meaning?

'Yes...' If her cheeks had been hot before, now she felt flames consuming her.

The night air was warm and scented, but it cooled her burning cheeks during the drive back in the open car.

'You will move into a room nearer to mine tonight.'

Christian's cool, flat announcement made her jerk her head round in alarm. They'd crunched to a halt in the pebbled courtyard, stepped out of the Mercedes, and were standing in the lamplit darkness.

'Whatever for?'

'For your safety, Emily.'

'Oh...!' Thrown into confusion, she searched her shattered thoughts. 'You think Greg Vernon might come creeping back to finish what he tried to start?' She was half joking, but somehow the words came out with a more serious ring than she'd intended.

'It is possible.' Christian's voice was hard as steel.

'Oh, I really don't think he was *serious*...' She stopped, suddenly feeling cold inside.

She stared up at the dark bulk of the building. A faint *frisson* of apprehension slithered down her spine. The Château de Mordin was an old, two-storeyed mansion built around three sides of a wide shingled courtyard. Its walls—what could be seen of them beneath dense green creeper, and between endless rows of tall, arched windows with wooden shutters—were smooth-rendered and white-washed. The shrill of the cicadas was the only sound.

For her own peace of mind she'd played down the whole Greg Vernon episode. Now, standing here in the eerie silence of the night, she felt her imagination fire into overdrive. An owl hooted from the vicinity of one of the massive cedars nearby and she jumped involuntarily.

Had Greg Vernon been seriously about to molest her? If she hadn't turned her hand to her bit of surprise judo, if Christian hadn't appeared when he did, would things have got unpleasantly or even dangerously out of control...?

At the time she'd put the Englishman down as a relatively harmless flirt, with delusions about his own sex appeal. Now, delayed reaction was setting in.

Christian had turned to gaze around the courtyard. He stood with his back to her, his hands thrust into his jacket pockets, and she stared at him unwillingly. Tall, over six feet, and broad-shouldered, he had the smooth-muscled physique of an athlete. In profile his features had a brooding, hooded power. The trouble was, Emily acknowledged ruefully, that Christian Malraux exuded far greater danger than Greg Vernon ever could...

'I'll be fine, honestly,' she countered hurriedly. 'I'll lock my door. Don't worry...'

'You will move across to the room next to mine. Tonight.' Christian turned to gaze down at her, his expression harder. 'I have no wish to lie awake half the night worried that rape and pillage may be taking place across there.'

'For heavens' sake, there's no need for any fuss. I'll be perfectly safe! And I *can* take care of myself!'

'You will do as I say.' The deep voice held an implacable note, raising her hackles. Christian Malraux could be charming when he wished, but he had a nasty tyrannical streak, Emily decided crossly. She recalled his icy dismissal of Greg Vernon. Here was a man used to being obeyed.

'I'd rather stay where I am now!'

'Indeed?' One dark eyebrow angled scathingly as he studied her mutinous face. 'Perhaps I misjudged the situation? Perhaps, if I had not intervened, the outcome would have been very different?'

She stared at him in silence.

'What is that supposed to mean?'

'Things are not always what they appear,' he murmured thoughtfully. 'Is it possible perhaps that you were enjoying your rough session with Greg Vernon, Emily? And my appearance spoiled things for you?'

Anger gripped her. 'If you mean what I think you mean, that's a . . . a *disgusting* suggestion!'

'Is it?' Christian sounded unperturbed by her pent-up outrage. 'In that case, you will be happier sleeping in another room. Come, we'll fetch your things.'

There was little option, Emily decided furiously, but to follow orders, for the time being. And humouring her new boss seemed diplomatic, when she'd controlled her temper enough to take a calm view of the situation.

'Is the château always this deserted?' In a valiant effort to somehow retrieve the deteriorating atmosphere between them, Emily's query was made with elaborate politeness as they returned across the shadowy courtyard with her repacked cases. 'It gives me the distinct impression that it was built to house more than two people!'

She'd endured his patronising supervision while she collected her belongings. Now she felt a fresh stab of annoyance at his humourless smile.

'Before my aunt died, the place was usually packed with staff, guests, weekend parties. I imagine that social life tailed off these last few years.

The village *"fête champêtre"* is traditionally cel-
ebrated here. There is a floodlit *grand bal* here
in two weeks' time. That should bring a little
more life to the place... depending on the
numbers attending.'

There was that dry cynicism again in his voice,
which seemed to intrude whenever the château
was mentioned...

'But the business side of things—surely there
are more live-in staff than your housekeeper,
Lisette Duvert, and the occasional casual odd-
job man like Greg Vernon?'

'This is as my uncle left it. I've been working
on building up the sales side, but I haven't been
able to give the place my undivided attention. Too
many loose ends from my former profession. And
I have not yet fully decided on the future of the
Château de Mordin.'

Emily stopped in the doorway of the bedroom
he'd shown her into, staring up at him in surprise. 'You mean you might sell?'

He shrugged. 'It's possible. I have not decided. Six years ago, I had no wish to vegetate
in provincial France in the family business. I am
not sure if anything has really changed on that
score.'

For some reason, she felt shocked. She took
care not to show it. She hardly knew this man.
It wasn't for her to show surprise at his lack of
enthusiasm for what seemed to her an idyllic
goldmine of a place...

'This place has enormous potential,' she began
idly. 'I thought that the moment I saw it...'

'Indeed? I'd be interested to hear your views on it.' His tone was wry, far from sincere, she thought resentfully.

'Sure. Any time.' Suddenly overwhelmingly tired, she pressed a hand to her forehead, shivering.

'Are you all right, Emily?' Behind the implacable shutters of his expression, the smoky blue gaze held a hint of concern.

'I'm fine. It's been a long day...'

This was true. She'd been up with the lark at her home in Gloucestershire, flown from Birmingham to Bordeaux, then driven up here on congested French roads in the hectic July holiday traffic. The sight of the big, square bedroom just along the landing from Christian's suite, freshly welcoming in shades of blue and gold, with a door ajar into a matching shower-room, was enticing.

Emily suddenly realised that this window looked straight across the courtyard into the window of the bedroom she'd been given by Lisette. No wonder Christian had detected trouble and arrived on the scene when he had— once Greg Vernon had snapped on the light, the scenario in the bedroom would have been floodlit for all to see...

'You've gone very pale.'

'I think it's delayed reaction to that ridiculous episode earlier...' The brief smile she gave him was tight with suppressed emotion. It had only just sunk in how close she might have come to a vicious assault earlier in her room. And this arrogant individual had the nerve to suggest she'd been *enjoying* herself ...

To her mortification she discovered that she was close to tears. Spinning desperately away from him, cursing her tiredness, her emotional state, the wine, the whole tense, edgy evening, she willed him to melt away and leave her alone to weep a few therapeutic tears and collapse into bed.

Instead, she felt strong hands on her shoulders, and she was twisted into the hard warmth of Christian Malraux's arms, and held firmly against the muscular wall of his chest.

'You are trembling. Emily, I apologise if I offended you. You are quite safe here...'

The deep voice was cool, with a trace of anger beneath the surface. Was he angry with her? Or with himself, for suggesting that nasty twist to what might have happened?

She tensed, panic-stricken, rigid with furious denial as he slid one hand up to the narrow nape of her neck, casually and confidently caressing her hair. He stroked the back of her head in a calming, brotherly fashion. It could have been Ben, hugging her better after some minor accident at home. She felt herself relax against him involuntarily as the warmth of his body transferred itself to her.

And then, with no warning, the warmth subtly changed. Secure and fraternal it suddenly wasn't. Searingly aware of every intimate detail of the hard, clean-smelling male body so close to hers, Emily found all her reassurance vanished.

When Christian gave an abrupt, astonished expletive and crushed her harder to his body, she lifted her head and blindly proffered her lips to his demanding, exploratory possession of her mouth...

She parted her lips with a sort of compulsive curiosity. The exquisitely raw sensations rippled through every nerve of her body. His tongue fenced with hers, then plunged hungrily deeper. He slid his hands up her slender back and cupped her head, his fingers tangling in the short, feathery rose-gold curls of her hair.

Dragging trembling hands across his ribcage, she spread her fingers across the width of his chest, superficially going through the motions of trying to push him away. Her lack of conviction must have been pathetically obvious, she decided dimly, shivering as her fingers encountered the strong ridges of his pectoral muscles. She clenched her fingers into small fists, fighting her feelings with every ounce of her strength, but then of their own volition her hands slid to his shoulders, spanning the firm column of his neck, seeking the strong pulse beating at his throat, the texture of his hair at his nape.

His hair was thick and clean, crisp to the touch. His body, through the light cotton of his clothes, felt lean and spare, powerfully muscled. A fresh wave of fire swept through her as he traced the narrow indentation of her spine with one firm hand. He caressed lightly all the way down to her small buttocks, and with shocked awareness she felt the heavy shaft of his sex, confined by clothes but nevertheless rampantly male, powerfully and unmistakably aroused, pressing against the flatness of her stomach through the silk of her sarong-skirt. A shudder of need seemed to resonate through her, but alongside it came a faint return to sanity.

The shudder seemed to transfer itself to Christian, and with a thick curse under his breath he abruptly separated himself from her. One hand on her shoulder, he caught her chin with the other, to lift her flushed face for inspection. The smoky blue eyes were darker. The sleepy, lidded gaze was shuttered, and unreadable.

'*Je m'excuse*, Emily. I did not intend that to happen. I did not seek to light a conflagration between us...' His breathing was erratic, his deep voice was harder, but ruefully amused as well. As if he'd been taken genuinely by surprise.

'I ... you didn't ...' Her voice sounded disembodied. She was trembling from head to foot.

'Now I think I have frightened you even more than Greg Vernon.'

She made a determined effort to laugh it off, backing away and twisting her chin free from the disturbing warmth of his fingers. 'Don't worry, I doubt if I'll have nightmares!'

'Good.' He was smiling wryly now, a wary, watchful light in his eyes. 'We would not want any complications to hinder our working relationship, would we?'

'I'll be sure to lock my door!' she said tartly.

'That would be advisable.' His blue eyes held such a gleam of dry humour that it twisted a fresh knot in the painful muddle of her emotions. Some inner parts of her body she had never even known existed until now were aching and shimmering and melting, and behaving in an outrageously unladylike fashion. 'You're quite a little sex siren, aren't you, Emily?'

'I assure you I am *not*!' she snapped, incensed at his laughing mockery. 'And what a *typical* sexist male comment! Blaming the *female* for his own lack of control!'

'I count myself fortunate. At least I have not been immobilised by one of your terrifying judo techniques. *Bonne nuit*, Emily. *Dors bien.*'

She clenched her fists at her sides, opened her mouth to speak, but found it impossible. She was too choked with anger.

When he turned away and she closed the door on his cool, retreating lope down the landing she stood quite still, staring at the panelled dark oak door, filled with such a savage intensity of reaction that she felt like screaming and sobbing and hammering furiously against the wall.

Lisette Duvert woke her, with a tray of breakfast which she set down, none too graciously, on the table beside her bed.

'Christian said I'd find you in here,' she announced without prevarication. 'What happened between you and Greg last night?' She spoke in French, and her tone was decidedly unfriendly.

Emily blinked, rubbing her eyes, and struggled to sit up in bed, staring at her uninvited visitor. Lisette was an intensely pretty girl, with an oval face and the sort of ethereal pallor which men would doubtless find fascinating. Her eyes were as green as the sloping lawns visible through the rear windows of the bedroom. With her shoulder-length black hair and heavy fringe, and wearing a short, figure-hugging black sundress, she had a faintly witch-like air about her.

'Didn't Christian...Monsieur Malraux tell you?' She managed to keep her voice level, and polite.

'He told me some unlikely story of Greg bursting into your room and trying to molest you!'

Lisette sounded as if she had no doubt that Emily had made the whole thing up. Emily swung her legs out of bed, and stood up, facing the French girl. She was thankful for her relatively modest nightwear, an oversized white T-shirt with a yellow sun printed on the front. And she felt grateful, too, for the fact that even in bare feet she was an inch taller than Lisette.

'I gather you hired Greg Vernon?' she queried calmly. 'So I'm sorry if you feel upset that he was fired straight away! But I can assure you the story is no exaggeration...'

'No? Or perhaps you simply twisted it around to suit yourself?' Dislike blazed out of Lisette's green eyes.

Emily blinked involuntarily under the heat of the other girl's temper. 'What on earth do you mean?'

'I mean, perhaps Christian came back and caught you in an embarrassing situation, and you threw the blame on Greg?'

This was so close to Christian's cynical conjecturing last night that Emily felt a sick tightening in her stomach.

'That's simply not true——' she began furiously.

'On the contrary...' It was Christian's husky, cuttingly amused voice from the door, making both of them swing round. 'Emily did not throw the blame on Greg, she threw *Greg*. Over her shoulder.'

His dark face was sardonic as he assessed Lisette's dismayed reaction to his sudden appearance. 'Emily is a judo expert, Lisette. We shall all need to tiptoe carefully around her while she is working here.'

With a toss of her black head, Lisette gave Christian a slow, provocative smile, then cast a withering glance back at Emily.

'*Judo*?' she sneered disbelievingly. 'Greg is a friend of mine. *I* do not need to use judo against him! This girl was obviously leading him on!'

'*Ça suffit*, Lisette.' Christian's voice contained a razor-edge which Emily was beginning to recognise. 'If you wish to continue working for me, I advise you to occupy yourself only with matters which concern you.'

The put-down was cool and devastating. The French girl gave an angry shrug, glaring at Christian with such simmering reproach that Emily had to suppress a smile. After a fraught silence, she spun on her heel and marched from the room.

How to make an enemy in ten seconds flat, Emily reflected dubiously, left facing Christian with mixed emotions. Under that intense appraisal she felt agitated, horribly self-conscious. Abruptly she had no idea what to do with her hands. The T-shirt felt transparent...

'You don't go in for finesse in your relationships with your employees, do you?' She couldn't help it, the accusation tripped off her tongue.

Christian's face darkened. 'Lisette is a hangover from my uncle Thierry's occupancy. As housekeepers go, she leaves much to be desired.'

'What do you mean, a "hang-over"?' Clasping her hands behind her back didn't help. It only served to emphasise the thrust of her breasts against the fine jersey material. She settled for a defensively aggressive position, arms folded across her chest.

'I mean that I did not appoint her. And that, *if* I stay long enough, I may well have to replace her.'

Through the receding haze of sleep, and the distracting effect of Christian's presence, Emily felt she understood the situation even less than she had last night. Was Christian Malraux here against his will, as a reluctant caretaker of his family business, because of his uncle's death?

And yet last night he'd talked of his need to find an alternative career, to find something which literally 'brought him back down to earth'. What could be more ideal than growing grapes, producing wine? What could be more creative, more satisfying? So why was he so stubbornly unenthusiastic about his current role? She was intrigued to find out. He didn't strike her as the kind of person who did things half-heartedly. If he appeared to show little enthusiasm for his current situation, Emily decided there had to be a reason why...

'Eat your breakfast. I doubt if Lisette has poisoned it,' Christian advised, a mocking note in his husky voice.

She levelled a calm gaze at him, taking in his cool, muscular appearance in suede boots, denims and loose white sweatshirt.

'I may be fresh from secretarial college,' she told him succinctly, 'but I hope I don't have many jobs with quite such a bizarre beginning as this one.'

'Things can only get better,' he agreed laconically, turning away with a glitter of laughter in his eyes. 'I'll see you down in the office in half an hour. *D'accord*?'

'I'll be there.'

When she'd consumed the strong chicory-scented coffee and warm buttery croissants, showered and dressed, and gone in search of her employer, she was struck once again by the potential for tourist trade here. The old château seemed sadly neglected. Most of it seemed unused. There were endless possibilities, she decided, her brain whirring as she took in the dilapidated reception area, the unvisited cellars, the lack of wine tastings. Yes, there were plenty of improvements she could suggest, just waiting to be put into effect...

The office, however, when she finally found it, wasn't the dusty cell she'd half expected. It looked surprisingly well equipped. There was some highly polished antique furniture, but the contrast of ultra-modern computers. The room was full of sun, with windows overlooking the rear lawns.

Christian was propped against one of the desks, ankles crossed, talking in quick-fire French on the telephone.

'Ah, Emily...' He cradled the receiver momentarily, his gaze intent on her appearance. 'I'll be with you in a moment.'

She hesitated, then went to sit behind the other desk, studying the brand new word processor with interest, assessing her ability to instantly master its intricacies.

The receiver clicked back in place. She jerked up her head to find the lidded blue gaze trained exclusively on her. Her skin prickled in reaction. Immediately she became body-conscious. The nutmeg silk suit she was wearing, short-skirted, chic and businesslike, somehow felt insufficient covering.

'Well?' he enquired flatly, watching as she lowered her eyes and made a show of examining the keyboard of the computer. 'Do you think you will be happy working here?'

'Happy?' She blinked involuntarily, then nodded hastily. 'Happy' wasn't a word she'd use to describe her tangled emotions so far, but it really was high time she pulled herself together.

'Yes. I'm sure I shall be quite happy,' she confirmed evenly. 'This office is far more up-to-date than I expected...'

'You were expecting some airless cellar surrounded by cobwebs and bats?'

'More or less.' She felt a smile tug at her mouth, but if she'd expected a similar flash of warmth from Christian it wasn't forthcoming. Whether it was the telephone call or some other reason, he seemed even more tense and preoccupied than usual. The relaxed if cynical escort of last night's meal seemed to have vanished into thin air. The tyrant seemed to have the upper hand at the moment.

'My three months here have not been entirely wasted,' he said abruptly, 'although my uncle's illness meant the place was neglected for longer than it should have been.'

'I...I'm sorry about your uncle...'

'So am I. He was my last living relative!' There was a bleak flippancy in Christian's voice which idiotically made Emily want to reach out and lay a hand on his shoulder, comfort him. She controlled the urge. Last night's unnerving eruption had arisen from an innocent act of sympathy, or comfort, hadn't it? Being in this man's vicinity felt like walking on eggs.

She caught her breath in frustration. She wouldn't be intimidated by him, overawed, like a shy child...

'You said you lived with your uncle and aunt as a child? What happened to your own parents?'

'They died,' Christian supplied briefly.

'When? How?' she persevered gently, secretly aghast at her forwardness.

'Together. From smoke asphyxiation. They'd gone for a touring holiday in India. There was a fire in one of the hotels.'

'How old were you?' Emily found she simply couldn't help herself. The questions just tumbled now, irresistibly, off her tongue.

He shot her a look of barely suppressed impatience. 'Seven. They'd sent me to stay at Château de Mordin while they made their trip. So instead of going back to my own home in Avenue Foch in Paris I just stayed on with my uncle and aunt. And now, Emily,' Christian's smile was humourless, his tone deeply cynical, 'enough questions. You were right—you are commendably inquisitive. Perhaps not so commendable when it becomes personal. Save it for your job.'

'Fine. Sorry I spoke,' she said with a tight smile. 'Emily Gainsborough, reporting for duty. Ready for work when you are!' As a rebellious follow-up, she clicked her heels and sketched a cheeky salute.

Levering himself off the desk, he gazed down at her consideringly. There was a slightly bemused expression on his hard, dark face.

'A word of advice, Emily...' he began softly, a twitch of humour finally lifting the corner of his mouth.

'Not more advice on affairs of the heart?' she queried, wide-eyed.

'No. Advice on how to ensure you don't get sacked on the first day of your Foreign Office post in September.' The deep voice held elaborate patience.

'Right. Let me guess . . . Number one: don't let my new boss catch me practising judo in the nude on the point of introduction? Number two: don't let my new boss practise his hot French kissing technique on me a couple of hours later?'

The silence which followed this defiant humour seemed endless. Braced for a possible eruption of anger, Emily stood before him, erect and slender, huge brown eyes levelled on his dark face. Finally, to her intense relief, Christian lifted his hands and dropped them to his sides in a quick, essentially Gallic gesture, and then he laughed.

'In fact, I was going to advise against cheek, sarcasm, and acting too clever for your own good,' he informed her wryly, gesturing towards the door. 'But I have the feeling I was about to waste my breath. You will just have to learn the hard way. Come, Emily, let me take you on a guided tour, so you know your way around.'

Chastened, she followed in silence. Her lighthearted attempts at ice-breaking hadn't worked out quite the way she'd envisaged.

The tour proved infuriatingly hard to concentrate on. One half of Emily's mind was on the information Christian was relaying, the names of the château employees who apparently lived lo-

cally, the layout of the working areas of the
château, the storage and the ageing cellars.

The other half was absorbed in fighting down
the insidious attraction she felt towards Christian
Malraux, an attraction which grew stronger the
more time she spent in his company, an attraction which seemed intent on defying all laws
of common sense. Think about self-preservation,
she told herself impatiently, the dangers of getting
involved, of somehow forfeiting any of her independence while her own career plans were still
so fresh and untried ahead of her...

'And this is virtually back where we started
from. What do you think of my ideas, Emily?'
Christian was saying, sending her into a flurry
of embarrassment as he turned a quizzical gaze
on her, clearly awaiting a reply.

'Sorry? I'm afraid I drifted,' she confessed,
colouring slightly.

They'd finished the interior of the château,
done a complete circuit of the grounds, and returned to the ageing cellar, with its impressive
line-up of big four-hundred-litre oak barrels. This
was where the *pineau cognac* matured for up to
ten years. There was a display, beside an old
copper still. It showed the different stages of the
ageing process, from pale yellow to marigold-
orange to its final dark sienna.

'You drifted? Didn't your secretarial college
include a course on how to combat drifting,
Emily?' The deep, husky voice sounded
harshly amused.

They were standing very close, far too close for her peace of mind. Her throat dry, she glanced around them in panic. His physical presence was doing unspeakable things to her poise.

She met the lidded blue gaze with a fresh surge of resentment. No one had any right to upset her equilibrium quite so thoroughly. If only he hadn't grabbed her last night, demonstrated that super-macho expertise, she'd have been fine...

'No...it didn't,' she heard herself saying. 'It didn't include a course on how to combat the after-effects of kissing our new boss within three hours of meeting him, either...'

There was a charged silence. Her heart was thudding uncontrollably as Christian stared down into her face, his expression narrowed, his mouth grim.

'You found last night...disturbing?' he said at last, deceptively casual. The faint jerk of a muscle on the hard jaw betrayed his sudden tension.

'In more ways than one!' Overcome with confusion, she nevertheless found she couldn't stop staring at the clean, well-shaped lines of his mouth, and the cleft in his firm chin.

'Blackmail, Emily?' he taunted, an edge to his voice. 'I kiss my new secretary, so now she plays the clown, refuses to concentrate on anything I tell her?'

'Hardly. It wasn't a one-sided kiss, after all,' she admitted shakily, warmth suffusing her cheeks. 'And...I...I was concentrating on what you were telling me, most of the time!'

'I am gratified to hear it.' He was quietly sardonic.

'I heard all the technical terms, the...the *brouille*, and the *tête du chauffe*, and your explanation of how the cognac ageing process happens, the way the alcohol evaporates upwards, and discolours the outside of the roof...'

She gestured quickly upwards, desperate to change the subject. 'I loved your beautiful phrase to describe the process...'

'*La part des anges*?' Christian's mouth twisted wryly, 'The Angels' Share...?'

'Yes. That's so lovely...'

'Yes. Perhaps it is. So, Emily, in view of what happened last night, what would you suggest as a solution?'

'A...solution?'

'To restoring full concentration in our working relationship?' The husky voice had deepened.

'I...' She swallowed hurriedly, sinking into that penetrating blue stare in a way which terrified her. She dredged her brain wildly for a way out of this deepening intimacy. 'I don't know...'

'If I kissed you again,' he murmured unsteadily, a smile tugging at the corners of his mouth as he stared, irresistibly at the wide, generous curve of Emily's dusky pink lips, 'would I risk the Greg Vernon treatment, Emily?'

'I have a feeling that you ought to,' she heard herself whisper, appalled at her weak flood of longing but for the life of her quite unable to control it. Her heart gave an idiotic lurch, then seemed to tumble upside down in her chest, and her stomach turned hollow with desire as he crushed her tightly to him.

'I have a feeling that you are right,' he mocked bleakly, but then he bent to hungrily, almost angrily cover her parted lips with his own.

CHAPTER THREE

'How old did you say you were, Emily?'
Christian's voice was deeper, a velvet masculine
growl against her hair.

'Twenty-two...' It was a shy, husky whisper
as she blinked up at him, bewildered, her senses
rocked by the effect he had on her. 'Why?'

'Because I want to take you to bed, right now.'
The sheer male arrogance took her breath away.
'And at your age you have no business making
a man feel this way on such short acquaintance...'

Shivering with reaction, Emily wriggled free
of his embrace, glaring at him in disbelief.

'There you go again! Blaming *me*! I'm getting
pretty sick of your implying that I am somehow
in the habit of ensnaring every male I set eyes
on!'

'Did I imply that?' His dark, rugged features
held an enigmatic quality, half mocking, half
intense.

'Yes! Last night you even implied that I was
enjoying being attacked by that creep Greg
Vernon! Now it's *my* fault that we...we find each
other...attractive?'

The brooding face above her was unreadable,
but the force of his embrace had left her in no
doubt of his physical reaction. It had triggered

a heat inside her which was like no other feeling she'd ever experienced ...

Now, though, she abruptly realised that her words were painfully honest. Much too honest. She was such a *novice* at this ... but instinct told her that, even when faced with such a devastating attack of physical infatuation, you didn't lay your feelings on the line quite so frankly.

'Do we? Find each other attractive?' He *was* mocking her. She was trembling, now, struggling to control the dark morass of feeling surging deep inside her.

'Look, I think this has gone far enough, don't you?' she said tightly, folding her arms defensively and fixing him with a wide brown glare. 'How about we ... we start all over again? Pretend none of this happened. Pretend last night didn't happen ...'

'And make sure we avoid all physical contact?' His grin was crooked, and shatteringly attractive. 'I think I should send you back to England, right now. I don't need this, Emily. I should find myself a temporary secretary with a little less sex appeal!'

'And I think I should find myself a temporary employer with a little more self-control!' she snapped back. 'I don't need this either! I've no intention of whiling away the summer on some sordid dead-end affair, thanks all the same!'

Christian was eyeing her with an unreadable glitter in his eyes.

'Now wait a minute,' he reprimanded, a rough tinge of amusement in his voice. 'Dead-end, quite possibly, since neither of is seeking permanent involvement. But sordid?' With a nonchalent gesture he reached out to draw her against him again, and with her knees trembling she braced herself for a fresh onslaught. 'Desire is not sordid. It is as old as time, Emily. Making love, in my experience, is anything but sordid.'

Shivering with the intensity of her emotions, she shrugged, then wished she hadn't. The action lifted her breasts, with their tight, aching peaks, against his chest, plunging her into a new awareness of sensitivity. Her stomach throbbed with longing. Insanely, unbelievably, she wanted to feel his long, lean fingers against her bare skin. She had the most unspeakably depraved longing to feel him touching her...

'I have no idea what sort of man you are,' she said in a low, choked voice. 'But you French have a bit of a reputation as...as legendary lovers, don't you? It's all a bit of a game to you, isn't that right?'

He laughed, a soft throaty sound which rippled reaction through her body.

'You are much too intelligent to subscribe to such childish, crass racial generalisations, Emily.'

With a determined effort she pushed herself free of his arms. The steady blue stare was disconcerting. He didn't need to drop his eyes to encompass her trembling form from head to toe. With her eyes caught and held prisoner by that laser-cool regard, she felt as if each item of her clothing were being slowly, sensuously removed, each part of her body exposed to his knowing gaze. Her knees felt boneless.

'Maybe,' she agreed with a slight, despairing laugh. 'Anyway, whatever...whatever this is all about, I don't think I can cope with it...'

The lidded gaze had narrowed intently on her face. A light breeze lifted the dark wedge of hair from his forehead, and she watched as he abruptly pushed his hand through it.

'Can you cope with doing a little straightforward secretarial work, Emily?' The amusement had returned. The intensity had diminished. Catching her breath, she hugged her arms round herself and turned away.

'Of course.'

'In that case, let us limit our dealings to shorthand and telephone calls, shall we?'

'That suits me just *fine!*'

Stiff with anger, she swung on her heel and, conscious of that speculative blue gaze trained on her retreat, she marched, with as much dignity as she could maintain, back in the direction of the office.

It was an edgy sort of morning. Switching her brain into a calm, professional groove took up most of her energy. Christian didn't appear to be suffering a similar conflict of emotions. An almost clinical detachment seemed to come as second nature to him. By the time the bulk of the business had been transferred to her for processing, either by typing or telephoning, Emily felt wrung out.

'I have a lunch appointment in Royan,' he announced briefly. 'Think you can cope with the frenzied activity around here while I'm gone?'

The irony brought the first smile she'd managed in hours.

'The place needn't be this quiet, you know,' she pointed out coolly. 'All it needs is a little investment and planning. Then you could have a restaurant, a reception area for some organised wine tastings, guided tours of the cellars for passing tourists, in different languages if necessary, summer publicity events like barbecues...'

'I'm sure you're right, Emily,' he mocked, with a ruthless glint in his eyes. 'I just wish I had the gut feeling that my destiny lay at Château de Mordin!'

Chewing the end of her pen, she cast a rapid eye over the mass of notes and instructions on her jotting pad, then leaned back in her chair and glanced out of the window at the sunlit grounds, the majestic sweep of the cedars on the lawns.

'Where *do* you have the gut feeling that your destiny lies, then?' she queried finally. She felt genuinely puzzled. Did he have to be so melodramatic?

'As far away from this part of France as possible. *A toute à l'heure!*'

'Are you free this evening?' The curt query came at the end of an industrious but lonely day at her word processor. Lisette had been noticeably absent; Emily hadn't a clue where. Apart from one or two male middle-aged château employees passing by in the distance, she hadn't seen a single soul since Christian had left that morning.

She blinked up at him now in mock astonishment.

'Free?' she echoed, unable to keep the irony from her voice.

'For dinner.'

Given their cool agreement that morning, she decided that it was impossible to tell the motive behind the invitation. Did he think she *expected* to be taken out for dinner every night by her temporary boss? No strings attached?

'Oh, I see, *free*? As in, am I available to be entertained? Sorry, no, I've got cocktails at six, a masked ball at eight, and a sleep-over party from midnight on. You'll have to make a prior appointment for another night, I'm afraid...'

The wry twist of Christian's mouth just missed real humour. He seemed stressed, she decided. She eyed his taut, muscular height in denims and casual black jacket. He looked like a man fighting secret demons...

'Has life been so very dismal today, Emily?'

She frowned consideringly at her short, peach-pearl fingernails before risking a gleam of a smile up at him.

'Let's just say Château de Mordin is missing its true vocation. It should be a monastic retreat.'

Her flippant humour finally drew an answering glitter in the intent blue gaze.

'So you are a young lady who likes to "party",
Emily?'

'Not really,' she amended hastily, her cheeks
warming a little at the dissecting expression in his
eyes. She began to feel that familiar body-
awareness again, and squirmed involuntarily in
her chair. 'I'm half joking. But you must admit
this place bears some resemblance to the tomb
of the living dead!'

He smiled, briefly, thrusting a hand through
the thick spikes of dark hair on his forehead.

'Don't forget the *fête* and *grand bal*, in two
weeks. Processions, fireworks, music and
dancing. Will that satisfy your urge for
excitement?'

He was mocking her. The edge of sarcasm was
sharper.

'I am quite sure it will,' she agreed, calmly.
'And I don't have any particular urge for *excitement*, as you put it.'

'Did Lisette provide you with lunch?'

Emily hesitated. Had that been the ar-
rangement? If so, Lisette had deliberately forgotten it. Emily had taken herself off to the
excellent *charcuterie* in the village.

'There was no need. I got myself something.'

Lisette might not be her favourite person, but
she felt loath to directly incriminate the girl, given
Christian's icy reprimand this morning.

He was frowning at her, his dark brows drawn
together. 'Then dinner this evening should
make amends.'

She shook her head quickly with an abrupt laugh. 'There's absolutely no need to "make amends" as you put it,' she chided, politely sarcastic. 'I'm supposed to be here to act as your temporary secretary. You're not honour-bound to entertain me. I'm sure I'll manage to organise my own social life as the days go by. I have friends in Saintes, as I told you. Perhaps you wouldn't mind if I rang them and arranged to go over and spend the day with them soon?'

'Whenever you wish,' he retorted coolly. 'But tonight I propose to drive you around the vineyards before we eat. Be ready at seven.'

There was a momentary silence while Emily assimilated the arrogant note of command in his voice. A small shiver ran down her spine as she locked with that piercing blue gaze. The scar on his cheek contrasted lividly with the carved darkness of his face. She was reminded of that powerful arrogance she'd detected on their first meeting.

She *could* stick to her guns—flatly refuse. But Christian Malraux was not a man to take no for an answer, warned a little voice inside her. And dinner was just...dinner. No reason to suspect an ulterior motive.

'Fine.' She shrugged carelessly. 'I'll look forward to it.'

'So will I.' With a cool smile he turned and walked away.

It had been a simmering hot day. The evening held a welcome promise of a cooler breeze, lifting the dry leaves of the walnut trees as it whispered

in from the Atlantic. Emily, showered and
dressed for evening in a short peach and white
flowered silk suit and low tan court shoes, sat
beside Christian in the open Mercedes as they
drove along empty country roads.

As a morale-booster she'd sprayed her
favourite White Musk body spray all over before
slipping on clean ivory silk underwear. As she
had caught a glimpse of herself in her bedroom
mirror while she dressed, the softness of the silk
lingerie brushing her slender body had abruptly
revived the scorch of desire when Christian had
touched her and kissed her. She'd felt annoyed
by a defensive little shiver...

She was dressing up... but she *wasn't* dressing
up because of any secret attraction towards
Christian. This was how she'd normally prepare
for an evening out, whether her companion were
male or female. She'd always taken pleasure from
looking good, from the feel of fine materials, the
fragrance of perfumes on her skin. And she
valued the poise and calm, that tingle of well-
being, which came from feeling well groomed...

Having quietly shored up her mental defences,
she now sat back in the beautiful car and tried
her hardest to relax, to ignore the unspoken
tension lingering between them, to abandon
herself to the pleasure of the fresh air rushing
past the windscreen, ruffling her pale copper
curls.

By the time they'd done a comprehensive tour
of the vineyards linked with the château it was
getting late. She'd seen rows of neat low-growing

vines bearing healthy clusters of grapes, inter-
spersed with fields and fields of massive golden
sunflowers which seemed to cover this part of
western France, lifting their comical round faces
to the setting sun. Powerful watering sprays
soaked the fields. The spray blew on the breeze
towards them as they drove, misting her face
from time to time.

Now Christian parked in the centre of a plane-
tree-shaded square in the village, and came
around the car to guide her towards a restaurant
with a bright green and blue striped awning, and
white chairs and tables on a terrace outside.
Mouthwatering food smells wafted out of the
open door and windows. The sun was dropping
lower, turning everywhere a warm glowing gold.

Walking up to the restaurant beside Christian,
Emily found herself feeling a corresponding
warm glow inside her, despite her reservations
about her companion. He was tall and devastatingly attractive in black, his immaculately tailored
collarless shirt and trousers bearing the hallmark
of European designer origins, his hard good looks
and rather alarming scar drawing intrigued
glances from nearby females.

Twisting her fingers thoughtfully around the
strap of her small tan leather shoulder-bag, Emily
realised she was experiencing that odd feeling of
'rightness' again. Why she should feel this unnerving sense of belonging, in the company of
someone she barely knew, was a mystery.

Maybe Christian had been making a conscious
effort to be charming once again. Because they'd

chatted, as they drove, almost like old friends. Not just about the vineyards, and the *pineau-cognac*-making process, but about her life back in England, her family, her father and Ben who were solicitors in Cheltenham, her mother who was content to occupy her life with house and home, the Women's Institute and the church flower rota; about Emily's own deep-seated determination to prove herself equal to her brother, in terms of independence and a 'meaningful' career.

They'd even discovered some shared interests, like horse-riding and tennis, a love of travelling and a taste for hot, exotic food. By the time they'd got to the restaurant she felt almost as relaxed as she might with her brother, which was the highest praise she could afford any male...

'There's an excellent Mexican restaurant in Paris which serves chilli tacos with jalopeña peppers, which could blow the roof off a steel safe,' Christian grinned, ushering her into a seat on the terrace, in the last of the evening sun, 'But here in St-Pierre-de-Mordin the Restaurant Joubert always used to do the best fish and seafood in Charente Maritime. Tonight is by way of a nostalgic return visit.'

'So...how many years did you say you've been away?' She felt that stab of curiosity again as she accepted a menu from the waiter.

'Five.'

'And you haven't been back at all? Not to visit your uncle, or to see old friends?'

Christian's smile suddenly held that disturbing hint of bitterness again.

'I haven't been back at all.'

There was a pause while he ordered pre-dinner drinks—a dry Martini for her, a Pernod for himself.

'But *why*?' she persisted, when the waiter had gone.

He was about to say something when chairs grated abruptly at the table behind them. A strident female voice cut in on their conversation like a pneumatic drill.

'Christian Malraux! You have a nerve, showing your face in this village. I never expected to see you again!'

Emily swivelled round in astonishment. The speaker was a large woman in her late fifties, wearing a tomato-red dress and a great deal of gold jewellery. She had a hard weatherbeaten face and accusing eyes, glittering behind round gold-rimmed glasses. Beside her hovered a man in grey, of a similar age, but wearing a slightly apologetic air. Emily scanned their faces uncomprehendingly, then turned back and caught a glimpse of Christian's granite expression, the lidded bleakness in his eyes. She felt a kick of shock in her stomach, a sudden thickening in her throat.

'You are seeing me now, *madame*.' His response was softly savage.

'Then come, Henri.' The woman was magnificent in her vitriolic disapproval. 'We will eat elsewhere!'

With a mumbled acknowledgement, Henri followed. The couple swept from the restaurant and marched out of sight.

The silence following this extraordinary outburst seemed to vibrate with such ferocious suppressed anger that it was painful to endure. Thrown into utter confusion, Emily stared speechlessly into Christian's eyes. It was impossible to tell how the brief, ugly scene had really affected him. His eyes were shuttered, bleak as a winter sky. Otherwise his actual expression was unnervingly hard to read.

'Christian...? What was all that about?'

'Nothing. A family feud, which happened years ago. Are you ready to order? Or have you lost your appetite?'

The cold steel in his voice seemed to negate questions.

'I...' She cleared her husky throat, and stared blindly at the menu, struggling to compose herself, to gather her scattered thoughts. 'Yes— I mean no... I'll have the... the cream of sorrel soup, and then the red mullet, please. I always prefer fish to meat, and I adore the way the French prepare it...' She was gabbling nervously, she knew it. Catching her breath, she fell silent.

It was the worst meal of her life. She hardly tasted what she ate. Often highly sensitive to atmosphere, she couldn't rid her psyche of the hatred projected by the woman in the red dress. A family feud? What could possibly have happened here years ago which would lead to a vitriolic outburst like that? What on earth did that woman think Christian had done?

'Emily, loosen up,' Christian said finally, his deep voice tinged with harsh remorse. 'Or are you wondering if you are dining with a mass murderer?'

The colour surged into her cheeks, then abruptly drained away. He stared at her chalk-white cheeks in some consternation.

'Emily? Are you feeling ill?'

'No! But don't say such things!' she said in a small, choked voice. 'Because it couldn't be further from the truth!'

The dark face opposite her was impassive as he considered her in silence. One thick dark eyebrow tilted enquiringly, a tinge of humour lifting the corner of his mouth. He abandoned the lobster he'd been consuming with skill and apparent enjoyment, and folded his arms.

'How can you be so sure?'

'Because you don't have the... the *aura* of a mass murderer!'

'Don't I? Are you saying you can *see* a person's aura? Are you psychic, Emily?' He was softly teasing her, she realised, but she swallowed hard and stuck to her guns.

'No, I'm not. At least, I don't think I am. But I tend to be quite... quite sensitive to things like that!'

'Then how grateful I am to be in your company this evening,' he mocked huskily, the intent blue gaze demolishing the last traces of her composure. 'In the company of someone who believes blindly in another's good character, just because he doesn't project some black shadow around themselves?'

'Why are you so...bitter?' she wondered quietly, her heart thudding faster in her chest.

'Am I bitter? Perhaps it's because I've done eight years' more living than you. I've seen how ideals can be compromised.'

He was talking in riddles. He had no intention of confiding in her.

She left most of her *crème caramel* dessert. Christian ate some local cheese and then fresh fruit, biting into a juicy peach with obvious enjoyment. His composure had clearly not suffered the same battering as hers. Coffee arrived, strong and black and reviving, and then the meal was over.

They drove back to the château in uneasy silence.

'Join me for a brandy,' he suggested flatly as they walked along the landing towards her room.

Emily hesitated. Caution urged her to refuse. But the fraught evening seemed curiously unfinished. She sensed that Christian wanted company. So she nodded, and followed him through into the suite of rooms he evidently used as his private living area, glancing with curiosity at the big, high-ceilinged sitting-room she found herself in, long windows overlooking the courtyard. 'Was this where your uncle was living before he was taken ill?'

Christian turned from the drinks cupboard, pausing in the act of pouring. 'Yes...'

'Are these his furnishings? His things?'

'No...the heavy furniture is his. Mine is still at my Paris apartment. But most of the books, prints and the kilim curtains and sofas are mine.'

She nodded slowly, moving to the window to run her fingers over the soft tasselled woven red, green and cream curtains with their black geometric Eastern design. The overall effect was gloriously ethnic. Warm, relaxing, inviting. Trophies of Christian's distant travels. The prints on the dusky, ochre-yellow walls were a huge variety of Indian, Chinese, antique English, European. Scattered around on low mahogany tables or on marquetry sideboards, beneath pools of yellow light from dark, conical shaded library reading-lamps, was an eclectic collection of carved wooden statues.

It felt rather like stepping into an enchanted, sensual Aladdin's cave. Glowing ruby, emerald and gold. Embellished with patterns and textures. A richly embroidered Indian wedding arch framed the heavy oak door into a bedroom beyond. The door stood ajar. Emily caught sight of the huge king-size bed, with its brilliant jewel-coloured woven spread, soft gold lights gleaming on either side, and looked abruptly away. Christian's bed was altogether too intimate to contemplate...

'Here...' Christian was beside her, with the drinks. She took the brandy and sipped it, surprisingly glad of its powerful warming qualities. 'And the bed is mine,' he added, with a glimmer of amusement. He'd been following her eyes. Emily went hastily to sit down on a chair by the window, stiff with embarrassment.

'There is nothing intrinsically embarrassing about a bed,' Christian taunted softly, slumping on to a deep kilim-strewn sofa and swallowing some of his brandy. 'So don't start blushing on me all over again, Emily.'

'I am aware that beds shouldn't be embarrassing!' she snapped, letting his taunt get through her careful defences. 'It's just...just imagining what goes on in them that's embarrassing...!'

'Is it?' He studied her warm cheeks and averted eyes with a glitter of sardonic interest, 'Well, now you've really got me fascinated. Just what usually goes on in the beds of your acquaintance, Emily?'

She got quickly to her feet. 'Stop it! You know exactly what I mean, and all you can do is...is crack silly jokes! Excuse me, I think it's time I went...'

Halfway across the room he intercepted her. Catching her shoulder, he spun her round. His fingers dug into the softness of her upper arm, and she winced, glaring at him furiously.

'Cut out the histrionics and finish your brandy,' he advised her with a mocking, husky laugh. 'I think we need to talk about what's going on between us, Emily. All night, in fact ever since we first set eyes on each other, I've been getting conflicting signals. "Touch me, don't touch me." "Kiss me, don't kiss me"! How about explaining exactly what it is you do want, Miss Emily Gainsborough, before I go up in flames of frustration?'

CHAPTER FOUR

EMILY stared in frozen anger at the hand restraining her. Every antenna in her body was quivering with the urge to escape, but she felt riveted to the spot.

'Take your hand off my arm.' Her voice was low and controlled, but the hint of suppressed fury drew an answering gleam in his eyes.

'Do I detect a veiled threat?' he enquired, loosening his fingers but retaining his hold on her. 'Am I about to fly through the air and land flat on my back, like the unfortunate Greg Vernon?'

Rage was a strange emotion, she reflected dimly. It could either trigger the desire to yell, or strike you speechless. She opened her mouth, but no sound would emerge. Her heart thudded in acute agitation.

'I've never in my whole life met anyone as…as *insensitive* as you!' she managed finally, her voice shaking with her effort at restraint. 'And if you want to know what I think, I think the conflicting signals are just as much you as me!'

'*Are* they?' The deep voice had a rough edge of amusement. 'You mean I don't know whether or not I want to make love to you? You're wrong, Emily. I regret there is no confusion in my mind on that score.'

Heat rushed into her face as she read the brilliance of his gaze, the unmistakable male message contained in that piercing, all-seeing stare.

'There you are?' she picked up shakily, a triumphant lift to her chin as she met his gaze. 'You see? You just said it—you *regret* there's no confusion in your mind? You might *fancy* me, but you don't *want* to fancy me!'

'I find it hard to relate to this crude expression, to "fancy" another person,' he remonstrated with a quirk of his mouth. 'I prefer the word "desire". It is more direct. Less immature. It gets straight to the heart of the matter, Emily.'

'I'm not immature! And I couldn't care less what you relate to,' she snapped, swamped by irritability, jerking her arm free of his hand. 'And you asked me to explain exactly what I want, so I'll tell you—I don't know! At least...' She caught her lower lip in her teeth at the mocking lift of his dark eyebrows. 'I know exactly what I want to do with my life, with my future. I just don't understand my feelings towards...'

'Your feelings towards me?' he suggested helpfully.

'All right, yes! My feelings towards you!' Her face felt even hotter. What was she floundering clumsily into? But on the other hand, what was the point in pretending? Something powerful and mysterious and overwhelming was happening deep down inside her, and Emily had always been afflicted with a painful honesty. Maybe that was why she was so hopeless at romantic entanglements. Blurting out your true feelings on demand was usually guaranteed to send a man running a mile in the other direction, wasn't it?

'Go on,' he prompted softly.

'I'm not sure how to! I'm not sure it's possible to have ... to have any feelings towards someone on such short acquaintance ...'

'We form opinions about people within seconds of meeting them. We like or dislike some people on sight. Have you never experienced this, Emily?'

'Of course I have!' she countered sharply, swinging away and walking stiffly to the window. 'You're twisting my words.'

'You mean you were referring to special *feelings*? Feelings of sexual attraction?'

She sucked in her breath unsteadily, 'Are you enjoying yourself, making me squirm with humiliation?'

'No.' Christian's voice was huskily reflective as he walked over to stand behind her, rocking her fragile composure with his nearness. 'No, I'm admiring your frankness, Emily ...'

'My mother says honesty is the best policy.' Besides——' she was abruptly defensive '—I'm sorry I'm so...pathetically transparent. But even if I've committed some crime by finding you ... well, attractive to a certain extent ... and not hiding it very well ... it doesn't mean I intend to ... to let anything happen between us ...'

'You mean you don't sleep around?' he supplied bluntly, mocking her agonised attempts to express herself. 'Neither do I. Sleeping around is not to be recommended these days. And who said

I intend to let anything happen between us, Emily?'

'Then why this...this patronising interrogation?' she demanded hotly. Her insides were ravelling themselves into tangled knots.

'Because I'm not immune to your gamine charms, *ma mignonne*.'

The wry, teasing murmur sent hopeless little shivers all the way down her spine. He was smiling, she could sense it even though she resolutely shrank from turning to look at him. 'I'm no saint. Only an average, red-blooded male, Emily. If modesty will permit me to say it, my chivalrous self-restraint has been crumbling under the strain...'

'*Chivalrous* self-restraint?'

Whirling round in a red mist of anger, she forgot all about her embarrassment. She lifted her fists to strike his insufferably arrogant shoulders, to push him away from her, but found herself instead caught up and crushed against him, her arms pinned to her sides.

Writhing fiercely, she jerked her chin up to glare accusingly into the dark face above her. 'Of all the...the conceited, chauvinistic, arrogant, self-satisfied...'

He was laughing down at her, she realised, wriggling furiously but unsuccessfully in his steel grip.

'At last, an emotional response instead of an intellectual one. It is best to bring these things, these complicated *affaires de coeur*, into the open.' He grinned unrepentantly, his teeth very

white in his dark face. The jagged scar became
less visible when he smiled.

'Oh, is it? *Why*? So you can obtain maximum
entertainment? You're the most hateful man I
ever met...'

'To clear the air, Emily. Because I like you.
Very much. I don't want you running home to
England next week because our relationship has
become too...complex. All this suppressed sexual
yearning is beginning to wear away my defences,
and believe me, *ma mignonne*, I need those defences firmly in place.'

'I don't understand. What exactly are you
saying?'

They were talking in English, but suddenly she
felt as if he could be using some obscure language
she had no knowledge of. She felt almost faint
with confusion. Part fury, part misery, part intense, unrequited longing triggered by the warm,
hard-muscled male body fused so intimately with
hers, a longing which stubbornly refused to dis-
perse. Run home to England? That just showed
how little he knew about her. This was crazy. In
just forty-eight hours it wasn't possible to be
sucked so deeply into another person's powerful
personality, to be half-drowning already in her
own flooding emotions...

'I am saying that I feel torn two ways, Emily.'
The deep, husky voice held a wry tenderness, like
a rough caress. 'I find myself wanting you, *ma
petite*, far more than I have wanted a woman for
a very long time. Right now, I am filled with a
burning and despicably base male urge to carry

you into my bedroom and take off your clothes, and satisfy this carnal instinct to possess you... but my intellect, my civilised reason tells me that you are too young, too... vulnerable...'

'So you're saying you'd like to take me to bed, but it wouldn't mean anything?' she managed to query, with a shaky semblance of humour. 'Not surprising, really! We hardly know each other!'

'No. You are misunderstanding. If it would mean nothing, Emily, feeling as I do right now, I would not hesitate! It would not... present a threat. Do you see my dilemma?'

She stared at him uncomprehendingly, slowly shaking her head. Her heart felt as if it would burst in her chest, it was thudding so heavily.

'How do you feel right now?' she whispered shakily.

The dark face twisted with wry humour.

'As if I am about to explode?'

Moulded against her softness, she could feel his male hardness. She moved against him involuntarily, and the heat expanded inside her. It conjured a dizzy selection of images and possibilities which rocked her to the core. Emily found that she was trembling violently, like a small tree in a tornado.

'Christian...'

'Sometimes things get out of control, faster than we'd like,' he persisted, softly. He ran his hands slowly up and down her back, exploring the fine, slender lines of her figure, the deceptive fragility of her narrow bone-structure. He muttered an oath under his breath, his deep voice

thicker, as if he was failing to convince himself.
'*Ecoute*, Emily, there are a million reasons why
this is a very, very bad idea...'

'Is it...?' She'd meant to toss a cool, sophisticated quip at him. But instead the husky words
slipped out, leaving her as raw and vulnerable
and utterly bewildered as she'd ever felt in her
life.

Her pride lay trampled on the floor. The intensity of unspoken feelings, of physical chem-
istry, was like a hot, liquid drug replacing the
blood in her veins. It was as if an outer layer of
herself had been abruptly, painfully peeled away.

Swallowing convulsively, she watched his expression change, an almost blind look blunt his
appearance. Darkened with desire, the pupils
widely dilated, the lidded blue gaze seemed to
burn right into her soul.

'Emily...'

'I...I know it's too soon...' she heard herself
whisper, huskily confused. 'I don't even know
you. You don't know me. But I swear I've never
felt like this before with anyone...'

Inside she was dying a thousand tiny deaths.
This was unreal. How could anything be this
powerful, this...destructive? What was she
saying? What was she flinging herself headlong
into?

'*Dieu*, Emily, it is the truth. You don't know
me...' He muttered it raggedly, his deep voice
hoarse, his gaze kindling on her parted lips.
Before he dropped his head to kiss her it felt as

if he was touching her with his eyes. Devouring her.

Then, when the stillness had lengthened until she'd begun to think he was carved in granite, he lowered his head and kissed her, a slow, searching exploration with his mouth, moving with tantalising hunger across her parted lips until her trembling grew uncontrollable and he scooped her into his arms and carried her through the open door into the bedroom, laying her gently on the kilim-covered bed.

When he came down beside her, pulled her against him, the desire was instant, erupting with such ferocious intensity that Emily felt as if the world was spinning out of control around her. She clung helplessly to his shoulders. She could feel the lean steel of the muscles move beneath the black silk of his shirt.

'Christian...' She moaned his name against the chiselled hardness of his chin as he kissed her lips, her cheeks, her eyes, raked impatient fingers into the feather-soft curls of her hair.

'Hush...' The dark finger laid over her parted lips moved expertly down the pale curve of her neck, to the V of her suit blouse, flicked the small pearl buttons free of their fastenings. Parting the flower-printed silk, he uncovered the delicate lace of her bra, the deep pink of her nipples visible through the scrap of ivory fabric. He slid his hands down to caress the shy swell of her breasts, and she gasped involuntarily, squeezing her eyes shut as he undid her bra, peeled the silk away from her. She felt too overcome with shyness to

watch his face, but she could feel his eyes on her,
and she could feel her nipples responding, even
without being touched. The tight, aching tingle
was instant and seemed to spread, to radiate out
all over her body.

When Christian cupped her breasts in his
hands, smoothing the taut peaks with his thumbs,
her eyes flew open in shocked pleasure. Entirely
of their own volition her arms went around his
back, and she pulled him closer.

'*Emily, tu es si belle* . . . so beautiful . . .' He
lowered his head to take one acutely sensitised
nipple between his lips, circling it with his tongue
until it was wet and tight and aching. Then he
repeated the delectable process with the other.

'Oh, Christian . . .' It was a shaky sigh of disbelief. A hunger was growing, spreading from her
breasts to her stomach, and warming right down
to her thighs. Unthinking, she pulled at the black
silk of his shirt, impatient to feel his skin.

'We wear too many clothes,' he murmured,
with a low, unsteady laugh. He levered himself
back from her, ripped the shirt over his head,
and then propped himself on one elbow, an unsettling vision of rock-hard muscle as he slid his
hand over her flat stomach, down over the short
silk skirt, then slipped his fingers beneath the hem
to discover the satin-smoothness of her thighs.

Shivering with reaction, she stared at him in a
confusion of longing and apprehension. Dark
chest hair arrowed uncompromisingly down the
centre of his smooth, flat pectoral muscles to the
waistband of his trousers. With each small

movement, another mesmerising set of muscles seemed to spring into impressive relief.

'You're beautiful as well.' She smiled uncertainly, lifting her hand to press it wonderingly against his chest, moving it exploringly over his body until she felt him tense and catch his breath.

'*Emily*...' A sudden, abrupt urgency took over from the leisurely discovery. The gentle caress on her upper thighs grew bolder, hungrier, his investigation of her body more intimate. With a choked, shocked cry she tensed slightly, shaking all over. Then the swirl of dark emotion seemed to cloak her again as his mouth covered hers, his tongue delving brazenly deep and explicitly demanding inside the secrets of her mouth. She hardly knew what was happening any more. Hot, burning hot with some new uncharted emotion, she writhed beneath Christian's hard length, each new caress, each private place invaded shooting tiny explosions of awareness through her nerve-ends.

When he slid cool, questing fingers to dispense with her skirt, her lacy briefs, disposing of the remainder of his own clothing with expert haste, and she was spread naked on the covers under the brilliance of his gaze, she was too drugged with desire to protest.

'I want you, Emily...' The husky assertion was powerfully male. 'And you want me, I can feel you do...there is no way you can deny that you want me *chérie*...'

The exploratory finger sliding daringly deep into the tight, moist secret of her femininity made

her shiver with emotion, and cry out softly and
cling to him. Tiny goose-pimples broke out all
over her body. Lifting her hands, she laced her
fingers blindly in his thick, dark hair, and with
a low, triumphant growl in his throat he moved
to straddle her, levered both hands between her
knees to lift her legs up and apart, opening her
to his possession with the uninhibited boldness
of a hunter with its captive...

The sensual finality of this surrender tempor-
arily shocked her to her senses. Emily surfaced
briefly from the flood-waters rising around her.
Through the layers of desire and pleasure and
need rose the one burningly obvious issue she
hadn't got around to mentioning...

'Christian...no, *wait*...!'

With a soothing, intoxicating kiss he silenced
her, reaching smoothly across to a bedside
drawer, extracting a small, discreet packet.

'It is all right, Emily. You are quite safe,' he
softly assured her, his deep voice ragged with
humour. 'Besides, *ma mignonne*, I come with a
clean bill of health...'

'No...it's not...I mean...' Helplessly, she let
his male warmth and his sureness overwhelm her
attempted protest. The real world slipped away.
Only this microcosm of a world existed, re-
volving purely around herself and Christian, and
this miraculous, awe-inspiring, mind-numbing
pleasure he was creating for her, and around her,
and inside her.

When he probed her softness and then thrust,
finally, hungrily into the hot tightness of her, she

dug her nails convulsively into his back, gouging hard into the muscles, heard herself cry out sharply. The swirling, breathless joy engulfing her was so astonishing, so intense and all-pervading, that it was some time before she registered dimly, through a sweet dark haze of sensation, that Christian had stopped moving.

With a thick male groan he had suspended all motion, gone very still. He was breathing hard and unevenly.

'Emily? *Qu'est-ce qu'il y a*? What is it, sweetheart?' It was a ragged breath against her lips, the dark velvet of his voice sending her senses spinning even deeper out of control.

'I...it's OK now, really...' Her voice felt choked in her throat. Heat was suffusing her whole body, tingling warmth through every pore of her skin.

'*C'est la première fois*...this is your first time?' Comprehension dawned in a slow, disbelieving groan as he levered his torso away, searched her tense white face with his eyes. With a shaking hand he raked his fingers over his face and through the thick dark lock of hair brushing his eyes, his expression dazed. 'Why, Emily? Why me?'

'Because...because I...because you...' She churned against the bed, in a welter of frustration and mortification, tears stinging the backs of her eyes. 'Oh, Christian, I don't know... I don't *know*...but don't stop...*please* don't stop now!'

'You feel so warm and welcoming and tantalisingly tight I'm not sure that I could stop now, even if I wanted to, Emily...' he teased jerkily, lowering with immense self-restraint to kiss her damp forehead, to smooth back her rose-blonde curls, trailing tender, infinitely patient kisses over her temples, her eyebrows, her eyelids, before finding her trembling mouth with mounting, urgent hunger. '*Tu es folle, chérie*, you are quite mad...'

'Yes...I think I must be...' she breathed on a choked, despairing laugh. Then she wrapped herself around him, trembling with urgent emotion, clinging like a limpet to a rock, eyes shut tight, as the laughter died and the ferocious storm broke violently, inexorably over them.

Emily stirred in the dark warmth of Christian's arms, like a coma victim surfacing after the longest sleep of her life. Her head felt heavy, her limbs weighted down. A languorous lethargy seemed to have invaded every cell of her body. Summoning every ounce of energy she had left, she moved her head and turned to face him.

'Are you asleep?' It was an unnecessary question. The lazy blue gaze was narrowed, sleepy, but very much awake.

'No.'

'What are you thinking about?'

There was a short pause. Christian gave a low, husky laugh and gathered her against him with a lazily possessive warmth. At some point since their passionate, uncontrollable lovemaking he'd pulled the covers over them both. She was co-cooned in a warm, secret world, and nothing in her whole life to date had felt so right, so preordained...

'Unrepeatable thoughts,' he told her drily.

'Unrepeatable? What kind of answer is that?'

'What kind of question is that?' he rasped, roughly amused, sliding his hand into her hair and pulling her head hard against his chest, firing a hundred tiny impulses through her body as her breasts pressed softly against the steel of his chest. 'What a delightful little innocent you are, *ma mignonne*. My thoughts are far too lewd and de-praved for your ears.'

'Christian... please!' The soft reproach in her voice brought a tightening of his arms around her.

'OK. *Je m'excuse*. You want the truth? I am thinking wild, rather melodramatic thoughts, Emily,' he mocked. 'Thoughts like, ''Who are you?'' ''Where did you come from?'' ''Where have you been all my life?'''

She stiffened slightly. 'Don't tease me, Christian...'

'I'm not.' He sounded wryly humorous, smoothing his hands down the curves of her body, sending delicious reactions shooting along her nerve-ends. 'It is true. Until yesterday evening, I thought I knew all the answers. Now I am snatching at straws...'

Wriggling in his arms, an intense frown drawing her eyebrows together, she lifted her head and searched his dark face.

'Truly? You're not just mocking?'

'Truly.' There was an unreadable light in his eyes which bewildered her.

'Me too,' she said unevenly, her heart beginning to thud against her ribs at the unfamiliar wonder of the hard, hair-roughened body against hers, the unthinkable intimacy of this situation. 'But Christian, whatever happens... I want you to know I won't regret what... what we just did...'

He was silent again. 'Won't you, Emily?' he said finally, an unfathomable note in his voice. 'I wish there was some way I could guarantee that for you.'

A small chill, a far-off glimmer of foreboding, blotted out the glow in her heart for just a split-second. Then it receded again, and she slid her arms round the hard width of his body, feeling impossibly happy and impossibly womanly and fulfilled.

'I don't need guarantees,' she said simply. 'Relationships don't come with guarantees, do they?'

'You,' Christian said slowly, tilting up her chin and searching her solemn face with enigmatic eyes, 'are a very unusual person, Emily Gainsborough. I have no idea what goes on in your head.'

'I'd be ashamed to tell you right now,' she smiled, her cheeks heating at the answering gleam in his eyes. 'I could write to one of those True Confession magazines, couldn't I? "My new employer made a loose wanton out of me, in just forty-eight hours." Scandalous!'

'Take care,' he cautioned huskily, 'Talking like this will most definitely lose you your job...'

'What...?'

'Instead you will become my sex slave until September...'

She fought down the small lurch of dismay at the mention of their time-limit. It was a fact, wasn't it? In September she'd be moving on, taking up her new Foreign Office posting, careful to stay single and heart-free to qualify for promotion.

'Sex slave? I'm not sure I have the right qualifications,' she teased dubiously.

'I'd say you're overqualified, my sweet Emily!' he taunted. 'Never have I known such instant aptitude. What took you so long discovering the joys of sex?'

'Sex is no joy if the right person hasn't come along,' she whispered, suddenly shy and abruptly unsure of herself all over again.

It was on the tip of her tongue to say that sex was meaningless unless it was a physical demonstration of love...just in time, she stopped the impulsive words, seeing them for the wild, crazy statements they were... She couldn't talk to Christian Malraux about *love*. She couldn't start pressuring him into a sense of guilt, or responsibility, or, worse still and God forbid, *pity*.

'Lots of my friends lost their virginity years ago,' she went on quickly, pressing her hot face against his hard chest to hide her embarrassment, 'but I always wanted to find someone to make it...make it special...'

'Did I make it special, Emily?' The deep, grave query made her heart tumble over in her chest.

'Reasonably special,' she teased unsteadily.

He held her gaze, in a long, bemused, searching study. Then she caught her breath, her heart swelling as he crushed her hard against him, trembling as he caressed the slender line of her back, shivering as he splayed his fingers over the silky curve of her buttocks.

'It's no use,' he growled, with a shudder of desire. 'I had good intentions of escorting you back to your room, Emily, of trying to set a few controls on this...'

'I should go,' she whispered, feeling the heat erupting between them again and instead moving closer into the strength of his arms, 'It would be very... improper for Lisette to find me here in the morning...'

'Just as it is very... improper to want to make love to you again right now, Emily...'

'Should... should I go?'

His response was a low, deep laugh. 'No, stay... stay with me, Emily...'

With a small sound in her throat she wrapped her arms around him in the warmth and darkness of the night, and the night flowed on around them, silent and mysterious, as if the entire focus of her universe had altered in the space of a few hours...

CHAPTER FIVE

'THERE is someone on the telephone for you,' Christian said casually, handing the receiver across the desk.

'Not my mother again?' she whispered apologetically. Since she'd unwisely mentioned the Greg Vernon incident to her brother Ben on the telephone a few days ago, her mother had taken to ringing at regular intervals to reassure herself that Emily was still alive and well.

'No, a friend. She didn't give a name.'

Emily reached and took the receiver from his hand. She caught his enigmatic blue gaze with the now familiar lurch of emotion, deep in her solar plexus. Wherever they were, she could sense his eyes on her. Usually his expression was unfathomable. Occasionally she detected a kind of wry, bemused tenderness, as if her motives in presenting him with her virginity had both moved and baffled him.

Emily was bewildered too. For the past week she'd existed in a kind of perplexed limbo, nursing her secret feelings to herself, struggling to make sense of the force of her attraction to Christian.

The first night, when they'd made love again and it had been even more rapturous than the first time, she'd woken very early in the morning.

Christian had been still sleeping, breathing quietly and evenly, large and dark and overpoweringly male in the bed beside her. Trembling inwardly, she'd propped herself up, and stared at his sleeping figure for a long time, recalling every heart-stopping second of their lovemaking. She'd been utterly confused by her own feelings: astonished, half ashamed that she'd had the nerve to be so forward, so open last night, yet at the same time stunned at her self-control in not blurting out the whole of her wild infatuation.

The harsh, saturnine lines of his face, in the pale light of dawn, were only slightly softened in sleep. Even without the brilliant challenge of that steady blue gaze, the combined impact of thick, tousled dark hair, intensely black lashes and the jagged scar on his cheek lent him a piratical air. Even in repose, the power of his hard, muscled body, with its whorls of coarse dark hair on chest and forearms, was a disturbing force...

But he'd taken possession of her only hours before, with a savagely masculine hunger tempered by breathtaking gentleness. And she'd begged him not to stop...

Her heart thudding, she'd slipped soundlessly from the bed, gathered her clothes in the silver light of dawn, and retreated to the relative sanctuary of her own room. There she'd sunk into a deep, scented bath and mentally assessed her stiff, aching body, sore in places she'd never dreamed of being sore, yet with a stubborn glowing warmth of fulfilment spreading out from her centre, and tingling into every nerve-end...

And yet a sense of self-preservation had kept her from repeating the experience. It wasn't that she didn't want to...it was quite the opposite. She did want to, far too much. The earth-shattering feeling of giving herself to Christian had left her with a painful sense of vulnerability. If she allowed this feeling to grow any stronger she'd never want to leave his side, she'd be clinging to his arm like a besotted limpet. And she knew very little about him, but she knew enough to realise that he was a man who rarely opened up about his real feelings. In fact he rarely opened up about anything personal. All right, they'd discussed likes and dislikes, tastes in food or books or music or leisure activities. He'd managed a handful of highly amusing anecdotes about his travels as a foreign news corre-spondent. Mentioned his Paris flat, the lifestyle he led there, a circle of friends. But he still evaded her questions about that awful woman in the restaurant...

And that first night she'd arrived, and they'd gone to the restaurant by the mill-stream, hadn't he made it plain that he shunned emotional commitment?

The fact that he hadn't pushed her to share his bed again, that he'd treated her with this wry, wary reserve, as if he was quite content to humour her and wait patiently for her next whim, seemed to bear out this theory. She couldn't be sure. She was floundering in an emotional maze. She had very little experience in such matters. Her deli-berately casual, arm's-length relationships to date hadn't prepared her in any way for this situation. She'd discovered that she hadn't the slightest idea what usually followed such nights of wild unbridled passion. No way of telling whether Christian's subsequent behaviour was the norm.

All she really knew was that the strength of her feelings frightened her.

Emily blinked at Christian now, as she took the telephone. The tingling hadn't stopped. She felt it whenever she was within a few feet of him. This morning he was devastatingly masculine in dark trousers and loose denim shirt. With that lazy blue gaze moving on her she felt her nipples spring and push against the soft white scoop-necked Lycra body she wore beneath an apricot linen suit. She even felt the prickle of response in her stomach.

'Hello? Emily?' A female voice spoke sharply in French, 'Are you there?'

'Yes ... yes!' She recognised the voice, even though it was years since they'd met. 'Marianne!' She had a quick vision of her friend as she'd last seen her six years ago, a vivacious, worldly-wise sixteen-year-old, cropped black hair and shining dark eyes. They'd first met when Marianne's theatre workshop group had visited Emily's home town, and Emily's group had gone to France a few months later on an exchange basis. As a result, they'd spent summer vacations together since Emily was twelve, although they'd lost touch even by letter this last few years. Her heart lifted at the thought of meeting her again soon, of renewing acquaintance with the whole family, in fact. 'How lovely to hear from you! You got my message, then, through your mother?'

'Yes ...' There was a pause. Emily waited for her friend to speak. A slight tension was conveying itself over the telephone line. 'Emily, I have to see you!'

'Of course. I was hoping we could meet for lunch or something at the weekend ...'

'Sooner than that!'

Marianne sounded strange, tense, almost angry. Emily frowned at the telephone.

'Marianne? What's wrong? Are you in some kind of trouble?'

'We cannot talk over the phone. But tell me, the man you are working for—is it Christian Malraux?'

'Why ... yes, but why ... ?'

'I will tell you when I see you,' Marianne said in a quick, flat voice. 'But I assure you, when you hear what I tell you, you will want to look for another job!'

When Emily put the receiver down she found her eyes caught and held by Christian's. A quizzical gleam had sharpened his gaze.

'What was all that about?' he queried lazily. Leaning back behind his desk, hands pushed into his pockets, he looked so overwhelmingly attractive that Emily had to restrain the urge to fling herself into his arms.

'I don't know ... is it all right if I take a few hours off to meet my friend tomorrow?'

'*Bien sûr*, Emily. I am not your keeper.' The shrug was perfunctory.

Biting her lip, she added uncertainly, 'Do...do you know her? Her name is Marianne Colbert?'

Christian had gone very still.

The silence seemed to go on forever. Outside, Emily could hear familiar, distant noises, a lorry near the storage cellars, voices from the workmen. But the atmosphere in the office seemed to shimmer with some invisible electric charge, like the shaft of sunlight glittering on a column of dust in the air, sealing them into a kind of vacuum.

Finally, he said, 'Colbert? Yes, I know the family.'

The dry, bleak cynicism of his voice made her stare at him in mounting bewilderment.

'Christian—is there...' she swallowed with a throat which was tight with foreboding '...is there something I should know about?'

'That depends which way you look at it,' he said shortly, uncoiling his tall frame from the chair and levelling an unreadable gaze at her from his formidable height.

'Did something happen between you and the Colberts?' she persisted unevenly. 'Is it...it is linked with that woman in the restaurant, Christian?'

'Why don't you go and see your friend tomorrow?' he suggested bluntly, walking to the door with hardly a backward glance. 'Wait and see what your friend Marianne Colbert has to say.'

*　　*　　*

Tense with nerves, Emily faced her friend across the sun-dappled pavement table. They'd met at a café on the busy, tree-lined main street of Saintes. A cup of strong black coffee steamed in front of her, and Emily sipped it jerkily.

'It's simple,' Marianne said, with an abrupt toss of her short dark hair. 'You're working for the biggest bastard this side of the Pyrénées! Such a ghastly coincidence! It hardly seems possible! I haven't slept since Maman rang and told me where you were...'

Marianne had scarcely changed in the last six years. Except perhaps to become even more chic, slender and sophisticated than ever. She still spoke with her hands, her gestures quick and vibrant and eloquent. She'd casually dismissed Emily's admiration for her figure-hugging navy crêpe dress, with the brilliant silk scarf at her neck, as her 'uniform' for the travel agent where she worked. Emily found herself thinking how extraordinary it was that they could just take up again where they'd left off, as if the time-lapse hadn't occurred. Perhaps spending five summers together, from the formative age of twelve, formed a strong bond...

Except that the mystery over Christian hung over their meeting like a dark cloud.

'You'll have to be a little more specific, Marianne,' Emily suggested with forced politeness. Inside she was silently seething with anger, directed at no one in particular, and all the more soul-destroying for the confusion. Christian had curtly announced an appointment last night, disappeared before dinner, and he hadn't come back to the château before Emily fell asleep. This morning he'd been up and gone before breakfast. Any hopes she'd had of dragging the truth out of him had been thwarted.

'You want the whole sordid story?' Marianne demanded, with a short nod. 'OK, you'll hear it. In just a matter of weeks, Christian Malraux tore our whole family apart. He wrecked our lives . . .'

'Hold on!' Emily clicked her cup back on her saucer with numb fingers, glaring resentfully at her friend. 'This sounds melodramatic, Marianne . . .'

'Remember Marie-Claire? And Mathieu?'

'Of course.' Marie-Claire was Marianne's sister, four years older. Mathieu was her brother, two years younger.

'Because of Christian, Marie-Claire tried to kill herself,' Marianne told her softly, her eyes narrowing in angry memory. 'And because of Christian, Mathieu might just as well be dead!'

Emily ran her fingers impatiently over her forehead. They were trembling, she noted absently. Tilting a wry eyebrow at her friend, she attempted a smile. Her stomach felt hollow with fear.

'You're not getting any easier to follow.'

'All right. Our family and the Malraux family were friends. Old friends. Marie-Claire fell in love with Christian. She thought he felt the same way, especially after he asked her to marry him. Instead he jilted her just a week before their wedding. She took an overdose. Luckily we found her before she died . . . and then Mathieu . . .'

Emily's hands were gripped together in her lap, so tightly her knuckles were white.

'Go on . . .' she managed faintly.

'Mathieu adored Marie-Claire. He was so upset he went to see Christian, one night. At the Château. Christian had been drinking heavily. He drove Mathieu home so recklessly that they hit an oncoming car. The passenger in the other car was hurt. The other driver was knocked unconscious. Mathieu's spine was injured—irreparably. He's been in a wheelchair ever since.'

Almost without realising it, Emily was slowly shaking her head. A chill, sick feeling was spreading through her stomach, creeping up to her heart.

'Marianne, I can see why you're so . . . bitter and angry. But I can't believe that Christian would do such a thing . . .'

Her friend narrowed an impatient look across the café table.

'Why not? I assure you it's the truth! Everyone within a ten mile radius of Château de Mordin knows it's the truth. Why should you question it?'

'Because, having met Christian, I . . .'

'But you've only known him a week!' Marianne cut in dismissively, tapping elegant fuchsia-pink nails against the side of her cup. 'How did you get the job there, anyway?'

'Through my French tutor, Jean-Paul Bernard, at secretarial college. He knew Christian

Malraux—I think he said they'd attended an intensive language course in London together—you know, where you're taught the language at high speed in a month? Anyway, he knew Christian Malraux needed a temporary secretary while he came back to take over the château. And he knew I wanted a temporary job to fill in time before starting work in the British embassy in Paris in September. So he fixed this up for me...but listen, Marianne, knowing Christian, I just find it impossible to believe that...'

'You're not actually standing up for him, are you?' Marianne demanded. Astonished dark brown eyes narrowed on Emily's flushed face. A glimmer of incredulous comprehension dawned. It was the French girl's turn to flush, a stain of anger suffusing her olive skin. 'Emily? What is going on? Do you find him attractive? Is that it? You have already formed some kind of *relationship* with him?'

With a superhuman effort Emily kept her wide gold-brown gaze fixed levelly on Marianne's. She'd always felt far less sophisticated than Marianne. Never more so than now. The look of worldly-wise knowledge on the other girl's face made her inwardly wince.

'That's really none of your business, Marianne,' she said with soft dignity, although her voice trembled slightly as she spoke.

'You have! *Mais, c'est pas vrai! C'est pas possible!*' Marianne was staring at her in horror, as if she were a freak. 'I know he is very good-looking, I know that he is physically very, very attractive, but...*alors*, Emily, be warned! He is no good! He is not to be trusted, he has *mauvais caractère*! Surely you can see that now?'

'I...I can't tell you how sorry I am to hear about Mathieu.' Emily found herself doggedly evading Marianne's pointed interrogation. 'And Marie-Claire, of course. What...I mean, how is she now?'

'She is married to a rich banker.' Marianne sounded stiff with displeasure at her deliberate evasion. 'They live in Jersey...'

'I'm glad. Things have worked out for her, then...'

'No thanks to Christian Malraux...!'

'How about Mathieu? How does he cope?' Emily forced herself to ask the questions calmly, even though she felt inwardly devastated.

'He lives at home, with Maman and Papa,' Marianne spat bitterly. 'Imagine! He is twenty now. Unable to live a normal life. For two years his memory was damaged too. He could hardly speak...' Marianne leaned forward, her gaze intent, 'The worst thing of all was that Mathieu *idolised* Christian. Christian was his hero! The adventurer, the traveller, the one who'd been to dangerous places, done exciting things! The man he wanted to be like, when he grew up. That was why he was so shattered by Christian's treatment of Marie-Claire. Mathieu had to accept that his hero had feet of clay! And then, the car crash...'

'You tell me to "imagine",' Emily said slowly, painfully. 'I can imagine how bitter you must feel. But surely...relationships fail, engagements get broken, for lots of different reasons—accidents happen—you can't hold someone guilty for the rest of their life?'

'No? *Ecoute*, Emily, the Malrauxes were always much richer than we were. And yet, with all the Malraux money, that bastard Christian has never once offered to pay compensation, to help Mathieu financially... he didn't care, he moved away to Paris, travelled abroad! Kept well out of the way. Until now! I can't believe he's had the nerve to come back to St-Pierre-de-Mordin! And I can't believe that you are sitting there, sticking up for that man!'

Emily couldn't listen any more. She felt as if she were hearing accusations about a stranger, someone she couldn't possibly know. Marianne was branding Christian Malraux the worst kind of selfish, reckless, callous brute...

And yet she'd trusted him instinctively, trusted him so deeply that she'd surrendered to him, physically and emotionally, within forty-eight hours of meeting him...

Not merely surrendered, but practically thrown herself into his bed...

Was she misguided and blinded by infatuation? Normally she was intuitive about character. She was sensitive. She somehow sensed good or bad in people. But she'd never fallen dramatically under a man's spell before. She'd never found herself with the ground knocked abruptly from under her feet, with every moral value overturned in a single night. She'd never felt so churned up inside over anyone in her life...

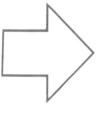

NO COST! NO OBLIGATION TO BUY!
NO PURCHASE NECESSARY!

PLAY "LUCKY 7" AND GET FIVE FREE GIFTS!

HOW TO PLAY:

1. With a coin, carefully scratch off the silver box at the right. Then check the claim chart to see what we have for you — FREE BOOKS and a gift — ALL YOURS! ALL FREE!

2. Send back this card and you'll receive brand-new Harlequin Presents® novels. These books have a cover price of $3.75 each, but they are yours to keep absolutely free.

3. There's no catch. You're under no obligation to buy anything. We charge nothing — ZERO — for your first shipment. And you don't have to make any minimum number of purchases — not even one!

4. The fact is thousands of readers enjoy receiving books by mail from the Harlequin Reader Service®. They like the convenience of home delivery . . . they like getting the best new novels months before they're available in stores . . . and they love our discount prices!

5. We hope that after receiving your free books you'll want to remain a subscriber. But the choice is yours — to continue or cancel, anytime at all! So why not take us up on our invitation, with no risk of any kind. You'll be glad you did!

You'll love this plush, cuddly Teddy Bear, an adorable accessory for your dressing table, bookcase or desk. Measuring 5½" tall, he's soft and brown and has a bright red ribbon around his neck—he's completely captivating! And he's yours absolutely free, when you accept this no-risk offer!

PLAY "LUCKY 7"

**Just scratch off the silver box with a coin.
Then check below to see the gifts you get.**

YES! I have scratched off the silver box. Please send me all the gifts for which I qualify. I understand I am under no obligation to purchase any books, as explained on the back and on the opposite page.

306 CIH ASYW
(C-H-P-02/95)

NAME

ADDRESS   APT.

CITY   PROVINCE   POSTAL CODE

7	7	7	**WORTH FOUR FREE BOOKS PLUS A FREE CUDDLY TEDDY BEAR**
🍒	🍒	🍒	**WORTH THREE FREE BOOKS**
●	●	●	**WORTH TWO FREE BOOKS**
🔔	🔔	🍒	**WORTH ONE FREE BOOK**

Offer limited to one per household and not valid to current Harlequin Presents® subscribers. All orders subject to approval.

THE HARLEQUIN READER SERVICE®: HERE'S HOW IT WORKS

Accepting free books places you under no obligation to buy anything. You may keep the books and gift and return the shipping statement marked "cancel". If you do not cancel, about a month later we'll send you 6 additional novels, and bill you just $2.74 each plus 25¢ delivery and GST*. That's the complete price and—compared to cover prices of $3.75 each—quite a bargain! You may cancel at any time, but if you choose to continue, every month we'll send you 6 more books, which you may either purchase at the discount price...or return at our expense and cancel your subscription.

*Terms and prices subject to change without notice.
Canadian residents will be charged applicable provincial taxes and GST.

If offer card is missing, write to: Harlequin Reader Service, P.O. Box 609, Fort Erie, Ontario L2A 5X3

0195619199-L2A5X3-BR01

HARLEQUIN READER SERVICE
PO BOX 609
FORT ERIE ONT
L2A 9Z9

MAIL▶POSTE
Canada Post Corporation / Société canadienne des postes
Postage paid   Port payé
if mailed in Canada   si posté au Canada

Business   Réponse
Reply   d'affaires

0195619199   01

Driving back from Saintes, she tried unsuccessfully to get a logical slant on the whole thing. What would Ben think of it? No comfort there. She could easily imagine what he would think of it. Her brother had always teasingly maintained that she was in for a major shock the moment she stepped free of the secure environment of home. Impulsive, unpredictable little Emily, clowning her way through adolescence, dreaming her way through university, her happy-go-lucky style masking her strong streak of independence and determination, and now out on the loose, in charge of her own destiny...

Destiny... Christian had said his destiny lay far away from this part of France. Those had been his cryptic words that morning in the office... was that because of this ugly thing with the Colberts? Was that why he was so ambivalent about his future, about his plans for the château?

Swerving abruptly to avoid an oncoming car, its horn blaring furiously, she realised with a prickle of horror that she'd been wrapped up in her thoughts and driving on the wrong side of the road. Pulling herself sternly together, she concentrated with elaborate attention on getting herself safely back to the little village of St-Pierre-de-Mordin. Once in the tree-shaded square, she parked the Renault and climbed shakily out, making for the bright red tables of the little pavement café. She needed time to compose herself before coming face to face with Christian again...

Ordering a *citron pressé*, she wiped damp palms along the striped cream and beige linen of her skirt, then hugged her hands under her armpits to stop them from trembling. Unseeing, she stared across the dusty square, at the high, waving pink trumpet-flowers of the hollyhocks which grew wild almost everywhere. The sun was hot on her face. She fumbled in her shoulder-bag for sunglasses, slid them on, took a shaky sip of her drink.

A figure was walking down the road opposite, growing closer. A brown-haired man, with a large rucksack on his back. Recognition jolted her out of her preoccupied misery. Greg Vernon was ambling towards her. A welcoming grin crinkled his face as he saw her. Emily wasn't sure whether to be amused or annoyed at the man's thick-skinned attitude.

'Hello, there!' he called, weaving through the tables. 'Mind if I join you?'

'Do I have any choice?'

'I'll say you do! I don't fancy getting myself up-ended again, thanks all the same.'

She shot him a wry look as he pulled out a chair and gingerly sat down.

'You should be safe enough if you behave yourself!' she laughed shortly.

'No problem. Scout's honour. Friends?'

She shrugged, and managed a light nod. 'Conditionally. I can't pretend I've totally forgiven you for your behaviour in my room, but I'm prepared to be civil if you are. Did you find yourself another job around here?'

'Yup. Helping on a farm just outside the village. And there'll be other odd jobs to do, with this village fête coming up...' The bold gaze moved over her slender arms in the sleeveless cream cotton blouse, and he shook his head disbelievingly. 'I still can't believe you threw me up the air like that! Don't you need bulging great muscles to do that? You look like a breath of wind would knock you over!'

'It's technique, not brawn. I believe in females having the ability to defend themselves.'

'Right. Point taken. What are you doing here all on your own? Taking a respite from the Great Dictator?'

'If you're referring to Christian Malraux, he's hardly that!'

'No?' Greg Vernon's rumpled brown hair and ruddy complexion gave him such an innocent, innocuous air that Emily found it hard to believe she'd allowed herself to be frightened by him. 'Oh, well, I gather he's different when it comes to the ladies!'

Emily felt herself go very still. Carelessly, she studied Greg's face through the smoked lenses of her sunglasses.

'Oh? What makes you say that?'

'I have my informants.' Greg twisted his mouth ruefully. 'I also thought I had a chance with Lisette...' He paused to order himself a beer as the waitress appeared.

'Where did you meet Lisette?'

'Here in this very café. I was looking for temporary work and I got chatting to her, just the way I'm chatting to you now,' Greg risked a leer which Emily deliberately stonewalled. 'I thought I was well in when she offered me the job at the château. Not so. Seems she's already spoken for, by the great man himself.'

Emily was beginning to think there must be some malevolent hobgoblin following her around today, spreading cruel rumours. With a lurch of dismay in her stomach, she took a shuddering gulp of her drink and stared into Greg's hazel eyes.

'Spoken for...?' she echoed in a choked voice.

'She and Malraux are lovers. I should have realised. Live-in housekeeper—I mean, the job specification is a joke in itself!'

'Who told you?' The question came out more sharply than she'd intended. She couldn't help herself. She couldn't manage cool indifference.

'Lisette...who else?' Greg's face had changed, narrowing to a speculative gleam. 'What's wrong, sweetheart?' He leaned across and slid a mock-comforting arm along her shoulders, making her flinch in outrage. 'You haven't got the hots for him yourself, have you? Take my advice, save yourself the grief. How about a drink with me here, again, tonight?'

Almost blinded by the tears prickling her eyes, she stood up, shrugging his arm away from her.

'No, thanks!'

'Shame. I reckon we'd make a hand-some couple!'

She made a dash across the square for her car. She was terrified of being overcome by emotion in front of the ghastly, gloating Greg Vernon.

Back at the château, as she made a desperate bolt for her room, she ran straight into Christian as he emerged from his apartment. She was still wearing the protective sunglasses. Catching her by her shoulders, he stopped her hectic flight, then after a longish pause he lifted the dark glasses off her nose, and scrutinised her red eyes and shattered expression. His own face was a bleak, cynical mask.

'Are you upset, Emily?' he queried, with ruthless softness. 'Let me try to guess what has disillusioned you, what has turned your naïve dreams to ashes. You have heard the story of the wicked, reckless philanderer who put Mathieu Colbert in a wheelchair for life?'

She opened her mouth to retort, then caught her breath as the open door into Christian's apartment was pulled wider and Lisette sauntered out on to the landing. She was smiling. There was a rumpled, tousled air about her. Her lipstick was smudged. Her mascara made her green eyes dark pools of malice in the whiteness of her face. The buttons of her black cotton sundress were unfastened at the bodice. The gleam of cruel amusement in her eyes was difficult to ignore.

'*Bonsoir*, Emily,' she purred, resting a hand on Christian's shoulder in a proprietorial fashion. 'Did you have fun in Saintes?'

Emily felt her whole world tilt into darkness and pain. The last vestiges of colour drained abruptly from her face as she stared up at Christian. She turned to go and he caught her arm, his fingers digging furiously into the softness of her skin.

'Emily, we have to talk...'

'Let go of me!' she whispered, her voice too choked to give vent to her confused fury.

'Emily!' His dark face was a ferocious mask of suppressed emotion.

'Don't *touch* me!' Her misery exploded into violent anger, as she wrenched herself free, shaking all over. 'You said I didn't know you...it's true! I didn't...I don't! I don't want to talk to you; I don't think I even want to *see* you again. And I must have been out of my *mind* to trust you the way I trusted you, Christian...'

CHAPTER SIX

THERE was a lock on the door of her room, but before she could slam the door on Christian and turn the key he'd put his shoulder against it and forced his way in, closing it with a crash behind him.

Grimly he surveyed her shaky appearance. He took a step towards her, and she braced herself for defence.

'Don't come any nearer...' she warned bitterly, squaring up to him with a bright glitter of tears in her eyes.

'Don't be silly, Emily. I just want to talk to you,' he began, narrowing the gap between them, reaching out to her. Gritting her teeth, she grabbed his wrist, fury and frustration pushing her instinctively into trying a judo defence move.

Abruptly she found herself outmanoeuvred. She was spun around on the spot, her arm pinned painfully behind her shoulder blades. Christian's muscular forearm snaked triumphantly across the front of her shoulders and neck, drawing her backwards against him and holding her there firmly. His masculine confidence enraged her even more.

'I warned you, I am also familiar with the martial arts,' Christian murmured in her ear. The deep voice was husky with a rich thread of mockery. 'Now, will you calm down?'

'Calm down? After the way you've...you've betrayed me?' she managed to bite out. His proximity, the warmth from his body, was wreaking the usual fitful havoc with her senses.

'Events of five years ago cannot conveniently be undone just because I made love to you a week ago, Emily...'

There was dry sarcasm in his voice. He'd subtly released the pressure on her arm while retaining his hold on her.

She stiffened, twisting round to free herself. She took a few quick steps back from him and met his level, probing gaze. In short-sleeved black polo-shirt, unbuttoned at the neck, and hip-hugging black trousers, his dark hair falling in its habitual tousled wedge over his eyes, simply looking at him was enough to set her pulses drumming...

'It's not...' She was about to correct the con-clusion he'd apparently drawn, then bit her lip. She was suddenly unsure of her feelings in any direction. She'd assimilated Marianne's tragic, unpleasant story, she'd felt shocked, horrified, disillusioned...and yet she'd retained a stubborn, idiotic little glow of conviction that somehow, in some way, Christian could not possibly be as black as he was painted; that somehow, in some way, he could not conceivably be the worthless person perceived by the Colberts.

Now she felt as if she was picking her way through a verbal minefield. If she impulsively blurted out everything in her heart right now, wouldn't she be setting herself up for even more anguish and disappointment? Wouldn't she be making herself unthinkably vulnerable?

'It's not what?' His echo was quietly calculating. There was a glitter of some emotion in the steady dark blue regard, but she was either too confused or too defensive to decipher it. She turned deliberately away from him, crossed to the window and gazed sightlessly at the gravelled courtyard enclosed in its high creeper-clad walls. In a week, when the village held its traditional *grand bal*, it would be full of fairy-lights, music, dancing and laughter. The inhabitants of St-Pierre-de-Mordin would be dancing under the stars. The old château would briefly come alive, perhaps relive the way it might have been a hundred years ago. Tonight, though, it brooded in silence. Full of evening sunlight throwing long black shadows.

'Maybe you could be a little more specific?' he suggested, wryly mocking.

'I need time to think about what Marianne told me,' she said at last, in a small, hard voice. 'I thought...that it was a very sad story. I also thought you must have had your reasons...for...for acting the way you did. I would never pass judgement on someone. But whatever...it makes no difference. I'm sorry, but I was a touch...*naïve* about the set-up here. I hadn't realised I was joining a...a *ménage à trois*!'

'Joining a *what* ... ?' The choked response
brought her swinging around to look at him
again. Christian's face was a study of cautious
amusement. 'What are you talking about,
Emily?'

'It's all right. You really don't have to humour
me, or play me along.' She managed to keep her
voice level and commendably pleasant. If she let
go of her iron control, the depth of her feelings
would be unnerving. Her passionate outburst on
the landing a few minutes ago had terrified her.
'It doesn't matter to me, anyway...'

There was a charged silence. She had the vague
impression that beneath his taunting humour
Christian was also suppressing his temper, or at
least tightly restraining his real feelings.

'*What* doesn't matter to you?' The blue gaze
held a dissecting gleam as he prowled warily towards her. He reminded her fleetingly of a large
black panther, cautiously stalking its prey, as if
he expected her to bolt away like a frightened
animal. 'Talk to me, Emily. You're not making
much sense.'

'If you are involved with Lisette.' Her voice
was unrecognisable in her own ears, delicately
polite.

'Ah. So that's it.' His eyes were still disturb-
ingly intent on her face. 'Jealousy?
Possessiveness? Already?'

She flashed a smile at him, arctic in
its brilliance.

'Not jealousy, precisely. Just a set of standards which obviously differ radically from yours! As I said, it doesn't matter any more...'

Christian's face was sombre as he moved closer still, reached out his hand to put a finger under her chin and raise her face to his. She had to clench her teeth not to react to the dizzy longing triggered by his touch.

'You have reached a damning verdict on my character, haven't you, Emily?' His eyes were grim, his voice harshly cynical. 'Maybe you have good reason. Listening to Marianne as prosecuting counsel can't have been pleasant. And naturally, to a man like me, guilty of such unspeakable crimes against humanity, a little casual infidelity means nothing?'

The soft savagery in his voice made her shiver.

'Evidently not!' she retorted unsteadily, something dying inside her. 'Seeing you together just now...after hearing what Greg Vernon had to say on my way back from Saintes...'

'I was wondering when you were going to tell me about that,' he mocked softly.

'About what?'

'I drove through the village a short time ago. You and Greg Vernon were having a very cosy little chat at the café. With his arm around your shoulders? No defensive martial arts in evidence?'

Emily stiffened. Her eyes were locked with Christian's. There was a dark flare of bitter amusement in his gaze. Incredulously, she realised that he'd neatly turned the tables on her. Was he really accusing *her* of pursuing a relationship with Greg Vernon behind his back?

'I can't believe this!' she managed at last on a shaky breath. 'I think this is where we call it a day! It isn't going to work! Suspicion and ... and jealousy and ... heavens knows what else, after just one week? I can't cope with this ...'

'I warned you to keep your heart to yourself, Emily.' The husky taunt stabbed silently and viciously home. Infuriatingly, tears burned the back of her eyes.

'Don't flatter yourself I ever gave it away!' she snapped acidly.

'Not your heart, perhaps.' Without warning, and decidedly without chivalry, he closed the gap between them, his hands sliding around to the sensitive nape of her neck, his fingers caressing the small, delicate indentation. A golden shimmer of response ran the length of her spine. 'But maybe what you gave to me was even more ... hazardous?'

'Christian, that's not fair!' The trembling was all-consuming. The feelings he could stir up inside her were clouding the vital issues, distracting her from thinking clearly.

'Why should I play fair,' he rasped, holding her prisoner, his hands sliding beneath the fine cream cotton of her blouse, 'when it's much more effective fighting dirty?'

'That's *despicable* ...' Her protest was softly fierce.

'No.' He sounded unrepentant, his voice a velvety male growl against her lips before he covered her mouth with his.

The kiss was deep, searching, utterly irresistible. He found the jut of her small, high breasts, spilling soft and vulnerable against his hands as he dispensed with the lacy protection of her bra. 'Not despicable...*desirable*...'

'Christian...' She gasped his name raggedly as he lifted her off her feet, and came down roughly beside her as he dumped her unceremoniously on the bed. 'Stop this...'

'You told me you would never regret giving your virginity to me, Emily.' He wrenched his black polo-shirt over his head, pinning her beneath his muscular chest with a cool bravado which took her breath away. 'So why be surprised to find that I want more?'

'There's nothing more,' she told him in a choked and furious voice, tensing helplessly as his expert fingers slid a trail of exploration over her exposed breasts, then pushed her skirt up to her slender hips with the boldness of a pirate. 'Christian, please don't...'

Her entire body was melting. Her brain was screaming in silent fury, but her treacherous body was melting, heating, igniting, firing under his touch. She looked up into his eyes, and read the dark, dangerous swirl of desire; it was a lethal combination, anger and passion. She couldn't think, she couldn't reason. The only reality was this quicksand of emotion, shifting beneath her, driving her arms round his neck, half drowning her in the depths of his eyes.

'Why are you bothering to appeal to me?' he rasped softly, fierce self-mockery in his voice. 'Didn't Marianne Colbert tell you that I have no conscience? That I am not to be trusted?'

'She said a lot of things...' Emily arched involuntarily, catching her breath as the seeking hands grew progressively more demanding, discovering the humiliating intensity of her own arousal in the warm, feminine secrets of her body. 'Oh, Christian, this isn't right...'

'No? And yet it feels right...doesn't it, Emily?'

Passion caught her up without warning, and she closed her eyes and tumbled headlong into the darkness of desire and emotion and longing...

Her mouth fused with his, her slender strength entwined with Christian's sleek, hard muscle, she stopped fighting and enfolded him with her arms, heard the small, high sounds in her throat as the sensations moved tantalisingly, irresistibly up and down her body.

'Oh, yes...yes!' The admission was forced between her lips, dragging a thick groan of triumph from Christian.

'Let me hear you say it,' he whispered thickly. 'Tell me that you want me, Emily. That you trust me enough to want me to make love to you, *ma mignonne*...'

'I want you!' she gasped heedlessly, her brain spinning, her heart close to bursting in her ribcage. 'God help me, Christian, I want you to love me...'

Her hoarse whisper seemed to linger in the panting silence which followed. Shivering and trembling in the steely prison of his arms, she began to dimly, distantly register that some of the force and aggression had gone, that Christian was deliberately cooling the wild heat between them.

'*Merci*, Emily...' It was a wryly ragged murmur. A rush of incredulous heat flooded her face as she realised that he was drawing back. That, despite the overwhelming evidence of his physical arousal, he was refraining from the ultimate act of possession. She blinked up at him in stunned dismay. There was a sheen of perspiration across his forehead, tension in the muscles and tendons of his shoulders and arms as he pulled back from her.

'Did you do this on purpose? Did you deliberately set out to...*humiliate* me?' she whispered fiercely. Shaking all over, she curled herself into a defensive ball as he twisted resolutely away and lay face down, his breathing uneven, his forehead resting on his forearms as he strove for control.

'No.' He lifted his head, rolled on to his side, studying her distraught face. His sudden, brilliant smile was lop-sided, and he reached a slightly unsteady hand to stroke her cheek with the backs of his fingers. Her heart seemed to squeeze in her chest, in spite of her acute resentment and frustration. 'Just don't tell me you never want to see me again. Not when you ex-

plode like a rocket launcher whenever I touch
you...'

'*Lust* is hardly a sound basis for a
relationship!'

'If we have any sort of relationship, Emily, we
need to talk about it. We cannot talk while you
are hurling accusations at me.'

'I can't talk about anything until I've got some
clothes on!' she snapped, her cheeks hectic as she
glanced wildly around for something to hide in.

Her wrap was on the back of the door. With
scant dignity she managed to ease herself off the
bed and make a quick snatch for it. Covered up
in the soft salmon-pink silk, she felt at least a
modicum of her self-respect returning. 'And what
on earth makes you think we can talk, just because you've demonstrated your great Casanova
technique again?' She felt close to tears. Was it
because she despised herself for her own vulnerability? Or because Christian hadn't appeared to
be sufficiently swept away by desire to carry
things to their natural conclusion? She wasn't
sure which was the most hurtful, or confusing,
or bewildering...

Added to which, he hadn't actually denied any
involvement with Lisette, had he? He'd just cyn-
ically agreed with her that he was capable of
anything...

'At least you have stopped trying to throw me
across the room?' His smile was bleak.

'True. Only because you were so damned superior in *that* as well!' she retorted bitterly. She
hugged her arms around herself in a welter of

pent-up anger and resentment. Unthinkingly, she
dared to let her eyes roam the length of his hard
male figure. Swallowing convulsively, she met his
eyes again. He was mocking her silently, totally
uninhibited by his nakedness. 'I don't want to
talk to you about anything!' She was trembling
inside. 'I'd just like you to get out of my
bedroom, and leave me in privacy. Is that too
much to ask?'

With a cool shrug he stretched lazily and got
to his feet, retrieving his clothes and beginning
unhurriedly to pull them on. He stood up to
fasten the zip of the close-fitting black trousers
with infuriating composure, then bent to shrug
on his shirt, pushing it calmly into the waistband,
his eyes level on her flushed face. Bending to pick
up her scattered underwear, blouse and skirt, he
added tauntingly, 'Now you, Emily. Get dressed
and we'll go somewhere less distracting.'

'Not in front of you! Get *out* of here...!'

'As I see it, there is not much difference between allowing me to take off your clothes and
allowing me to put them back on for you, *ma
mignonne*.'

Before she'd fully grasped his intentions, he'd
caught her by the hand and hauled her towards
him. Sliding the satiny robe from her shoulders,
he pulled her roughly down with him on to the
bed, catching her protesting mouth with his in a
deep, wildly erotic kiss. She began kicking in violent defence, but then stopped abruptly as he
crushed her mercilessly against him, because no
matter how much she hated him the intimate

contact was rekindling all those scarcely controlled feelings of a few minutes ago.

'That's better,' he murmured with ragged humour, subduing her struggles with effortless ease. 'Wriggling like that is guaranteed to get us both back in bed together...'

'You're detestable! If you think I'm staying here to be treated like this...'

'Hush...you're not getting treated so badly,' he teased thickly. 'You're improving your French. You're getting plenty of local colour. Play things right, and you may even get special privileges from your boss...'

'And I could take you to the European courts for...for sexual harassment...'

'Maybe I could lodge a counter-claim?'

To her fury he proceeded to slide her cream lace briefs over her ankles, draw them higher, set her abruptly on her feet, then hook the wispy lace bra in place with wry skill. Trembling uncontrollably, she found that the power to fight had deserted her. Christian's behaviour was a shameless display of machismo, but at the same time there was something so innately possessive and overwhelming about the intimate ritual that she could only stare at him, dry-mouthed. She hated him, and she wanted him all over again...

'We need to talk, but not here. We need a change of scene. Beds seem to prove a major hazard whenever we're together.' His deep voice was unsteady, the dilation of his pupils telling her that the renewed desire was far from one-sided. Reaching for her blouse and skirt, he

handed them to her and abruptly turned away.
'Since I met you, my life has been feeling un-
comfortably out of control,' he added, on a
firmer note. 'I've felt an inconvenient need to
bare my soul, Emily. Far more disturbing than
mere sexual attraction...'

Mere sexual attraction! Was that what he called
that fathoms-deep descent into emotional chaos?
Her psyche felt bruised and battered by the force
of the latest subterranean explosion of the
senses...

Her clothes in place, she caught a glimpse of
herself in the mirror and felt faint with shame.
Her hair was rumpled, her lips swollen, her eyes
huge dark smudges in her pale face. Lisette's
dishevelled appearance just a short while ago
sprang unbidden into her mind. *Was* Christian
Malraux an unscrupulous con-artist? Could he
really switch glibly from a passionate interlude
with Lisette to a near-seduction with Emily? The
acute stab of pain took her by surprise. She
almost cried out in misery and disillusion.

'I need to wash my face and brush my hair,'
she informed him tightly. 'I...I'll meet you down
in the office.'

He shot her a hard, assessing look, then
nodded slowly. '*D'accord.*' He went out and
closed the door, and Emily almost buckled at the
knees with the abrupt relief of tension.
Christian's presence in a room was a potent force.
Now he was gone, it was as if a powerful elec-
trical charge had been removed. And as if the
light had been switched off, she registered with

slow dismay. Splashing water furiously over her face, she lifted her eyes to the mirror, dreading what she might read there.

She'd caught the sun a little since she'd been here. A light golden tan made her skin glow with apparent health. But a tense, unhappy face stared back, brown eyes huge in their sockets. The soft bow of her lips moved convulsively as she gnawed nervously at the inside of her lower lip. Making a conscious effort to stop the habit, she drew in a deep breath then blew it out slowly, watching the mist forming on the mirror image until her reflection blurred, ghostly and indistinct...

She loathed him. She loathed him for what she suspected him of doing with Lisette while casually taking advantage of her own foolish infatuation... She loathed him for the way he'd just treated her, with such cavalier arrogance...

She was confused over Marianne's story. If her friend was right, Christian was definitely a man who took no prisoners, who grasped what he wanted from life with ruthless contempt for others. By rights, she shouldn't trust him an inch. How could she imagine that she *loved* him? The errant thought came into her mind, and she examined it in silence, fumbling for her tortoiseshell comb and dragging it impatiently through her feathery copper-blonde curls.

Had she fallen in love with Christian Malraux? Was it possible to fall in love with someone in just one week? People often claimed they'd fallen in love with their life-partner at first sight, didn't they? Literally seen them across a crowded room, and known that this was the person they wanted to spend their whole life with? She thought of that feeling she'd had, sitting beside Christian in his car that first night ... and the way she'd felt when she'd wanted him to be her very first lover ... as if she would gladly die for him, as if the world would abruptly cease to turn if she didn't spend every waking minute beside him ...

With a ragged catch in her breathing, Emily chewed her lip again, her brain in turmoil. She couldn't have been so idiotic. Surely ... ?

And if she had, then she couldn't stay here. Not with this crazy notion that she was in love with him. Not now that all this had happened ...

But she wasn't the running-away type. To walk out, admit defeat in what was intended to be a simple holiday job, would feel like the worst kind of failure. And it would raise all sorts of questions. Her parents, and Ben, would want to know why. And she had to support herself for the rest of the summer. She couldn't expect to find another temporary job in France immediately ...

The thought of home swam into her mind, a safe refuge. The big old Cotswold-stone house on the edge of a village, surrounded by rambling cottage gardens and a tennis court, with her mother calmly drinking afternoon tea on the terrace with her friends, suddenly seemed a very tempting destination. But Ben or Dad would give her one of those patronising, protective hugs and tell her she was a little home-bird at heart, fooling herself with dreams of a high-powered international career ...

That last thought strengthened her resolve. She'd stay, find the strength to fight this humiliating obsession with Christian. It was a pity it wasn't closer to harvest time, when the château would be buzzing with frantic activity, but even so there'd be plenty to do over the next few weeks. There was Christian's project on renovating the storage cellars, and having the ancient, obsolete copper still cleaned and polished as a feature to show to parties of visitors. And with the village *fête* and the *grand bal* coming up there'd be plenty going on...

And besides, who did she think she was fooling? The mist on the mirror had cleared enough to see her face again. She met her own gaze with a wry, agonising jolt of self-knowledge. She'd stay, even if someone was holding a knife at her throat, ordering her to leave. Right now her feelings for Christian might resemble those of the moth for the candle-flame. But there was too much unresolved. Too many unexplained mysteries. Too much in her heart that needed sifting and analysing...

She'd stay...

Christian was talking on the telephone when she finally made her way down to the office. His face was grim, paler beneath the swarthy darkness of his skin. The scar was a livid streak on his cheek. He was replacing the receiver as she walked in.

'I have to go to Paris,' he said abruptly, straightening up. 'Will you be able to manage things here on your own?'

'Oh?' Emily's voice wavered slightly, and she caught her breath impatiently. 'Yes—yes, I think so. But why?'

'A friend has been shot. He's been flown back to a hospital in Paris, but his condition is critical.'

'I'm sorry...' Why on earth did she have this sinking feeling in her stomach? Because of the prospect of Christian's going away? 'What happened?' she heard herself asking.

'He was covering a news story in Colombia, one that I started before I quit to come back here,' Christian's voice was bleak. He raked a weary hand through the thick wedge of dark hair falling on to his forehead. '*Merde*! I feel responsible.' He twisted a haunted, humourless smile at Emily. 'Marc has a wife and a baby. It would have been better if it had been me!'

The wry self-disgust made her wince. 'Don't say that!' she blurted out, all hopes of keeping a close guard on her feelings vanishing into thin air. She reached out impulsively, touching his arm lightly with her hand. 'Your life is every bit as valuable as his...!'

'You think so?'

'Christian...!'

'Sometimes I believe I have the devil's own luck,' he confessed shortly. The pain in his eyes made her heart contract in a sudden unexpected shock of emotion and insight. 'I imagine that there'll be an ultimate price to pay for these near-miss strokes of good fortune. The wages of original sin?'

She stared into his eyes, her heart thudding. She was bewildered by the mixture of black humour and some trace of hunted vulnerability which devastated her defences.

'Stop talking such rubbish!' she said on a soft, determined note, linking her arms round his neck and moving against him. An instinct beyond her control was triggering a flood of fierce emotion inside her. 'Your friend will be fine. I know it. And you're not a cat with nine lives!'

Christian dropped his head to look questioningly into her upturned face. While he studied her intently, he gently disengaged her hands from his shoulders, then took her face in his hands, his thumbs moving hungrily across her cheekbones, tracing the delicate shape of her earlobes. The thick-lashed blue gaze was darkly lidded, hard to read. But the smile tilting one side of his mouth was wary, bleakly sardonic.

'Come with me, Emily?' he suggested softly.

'To Paris?' She stared at him blankly, then shook her head vehemently. 'No! Oh, no!' She tried to shake her head, but the hard strength of his hands was overpoweringly seductive. It took every ounce of her will-power to resist.

'On a strictly platonic basis?' He made a wry travesty of a grin. 'There are four bedrooms in my apartment. You may sleep alone... in any of them. If you wish.'

'Why? Why should you want me to come?' she whispered huskily.

'Because I enjoy your company? Because I would like to get to know you even better?'

She swallowed on a sudden lump in her throat. She wanted to tell him that she felt exactly the same way, but events of the past twelve hours made her cautious.

'I couldn't. I can't,' she said stiffly, quelling the trembling inside. 'I need some time... time to work out how I feel...'

He slowly released her, his gaze disconcertingly steady on her flushed face.

'*Bien sûr. Entendu*, Emily. I will ring from Paris tomorrow.' He turned and strolled to the door, the casual flex of his shoulders revealing no trace of disappointment or emotion. 'Take care while I'm away,' he added, with a sardonic smile.

'Yes. I'll lock my door when I'm taking a bath.' The attempt at levity dropped like a stone into the tense atmosphere.

'You do that,' he advised, his tone hardening. The glint of glacial displeasure in his eyes as he left sent a shiver of apprehension down her spine.

Hands clenched into small, strong fists at her sides, she stared bleakly at the closed door for a long time after he'd gone.

CHAPTER SEVEN

'I CAN'T believe you're still working there! The whole family are appalled.' Marianne's voice was ringing accusingly down the telephone. 'Tante Mirrie saw him in a restaurant in the village. She and my uncle left their meal and walked out...'

Emily felt her patience stretching thin. When Marianne had rung and launched into fresh protests she'd intended to stay calm and reasonable, but her good resolutions were fading. She took a deep breath, controlling her anger and glaring out of the window at nothing in particular.

Tante Mirrie. That cleared up the mystery of the large, angry matron in the red dress, she registered, clenching the receiver harder. She decided against telling Marianne that she'd witnessed Tante Mirrie's dramatic departure at first hand.

Instead, she let her friend vent her bitterness, and frowned silently through the open office window at the scene in the courtyard. It was mid-afternoon; the air was hot and still. A bumble-bee droned sleepily in and out of the hollyhocks nodding their velvety pink heads against the wall. But the usual peace of the château was being shattered by preparations for the open-air dance. Fairy-lights were being strung up all around the creeper-clad walls and in the branches of the

massive cedar trees, ready for Saturday night.
Men in overalls were milling seemingly at
random. Greg Vernon, like the proverbial bad
penny, appeared to have got in on the casual-
work act with the local carpenter who was super-
vising the construction of a temporary stage for
the band, with much volatile temper and impatient gesticulations. Lisette, feline in tight black
cycling shorts and a microscopic emerald-green
halter top revealing a smooth white midriff, was
directing operations. There seemed to be an un-
declared war between Lisette and herself over
who exactly was in charge in Christian's absence.
No sooner did Emily pass on an instruction on
Christian's behalf, or suggest something on her
own initiative, than Lisette was countermanding
the suggestion with smug hostility.

'Emily? Are you still there?' Marianne's voice
had grown sharper.

'Yes, I'm here. Marianne, listen. Whatever the
rights and wrongs of it all, Mathieu's tragedy has
happened. Nothing can change it. And even if
Christian is guilty as you claim on every charge,
shouldn't time heal all this bitterness? He's not
a *leper*!'

'You sound as if you don't believe he *is* guilty!'

'He hasn't talked to me about it. He's in
Paris...'

'Oh? Who with?'

Emily forced back her temper. 'He went to visit
a friend in hospital.'

Christian had been gone for several days now.
He'd rung the day after he'd left, a cool, brief

call from his Paris apartment. His journalist colleague was still in Intensive Care, but happily the
prognosis was reasonable. He'd assured himself
that his friend's wife and baby were all right for
money and accommodation. He had some other
business to attend to in Paris before he came
back. They'd not spoken since. They'd had no
chance to talk, rationally, unemotionally, without
the spectre of sexual desire intervening, on the
subject of Christian's shadowy past. But, while
his suspected relationship with Lisette was still
too painful for her to contemplate, Emily had
found that she was simply unable to accept
Marianne's version of Christian's character. She
seemed to have a mental block where those accusations were concerned. She was surprised at
her own stubbornness—she'd never realised what
a sucker she was for punishment.

Sounding disgusted, Marianne let out a
uniquely French expletive.

'You imagine he will talk to you? You think
he would tell you the whole story? What an
innocent! You will be putty in his hands, *ma
pauvre petite*! *Ecoute*—listen! If you could see
Mathieu . . . Since he heard Christian was back,
he has hardly slept. Hearing that Christian is back
at Château de Mordin has stirred up terrible
memories for him. Before, he was coping quite
well. He'd even found a girlfriend. A fiancée, in
fact. Jeanne. She is sweet, she really loves him.
But now he won't talk. He won't even eat. He
has clammed up, in a world of his own. He has

a haunted look. Marie-Claire might have rebuilt her life, but what chance has Mathieu to do so?'

'Look, Marianne...' Emily chewed her lip despairingly, her stomach churning. 'Why...why don't you bring Mathieu over here? In fact, why don't you both come to the *grand bal* on Saturday night? All of you. You and your parents, and Mathieu...'

'*Tu es complètement folle, ou quoi?*' Marianne burst out furiously. 'Are you completely mad?'

'No, not mad. There will be lots of people here. You'd have the excuse of coming to renew acquaintance with me. It might be a chance for some sort of reconciliation...'

'*Reconciliation?* Why would we want a reconciliation with Christian Malraux, Emily?'

'I just don't like to see people I care about suffer through...pent-up hatred and bitterness. All this suppressed hostility. All this buried resentment. It's very unhealthy! It should all be brought out into the open and resolved, once and for all.'

There was a longish pause. Finally, Marianne said slowly, 'People you care about? So you really care about Christian? Yes?'

'I...' Emily felt a sick sinking in her heart as she faced the truth. Yes, she admitted silently. She did. She really cared about Christian. But it wasn't an emotion ever likely to find much fulfilment. She admitted that, too. The wild mutual desire between them was surely much too hot to last. Relationships based on whirlwind attraction rarely did, did they? And even if her own feelings on permanent commitment might have undergone a subtle, uninvited change since meeting Christian, hadn't he spelled out his own on that subject with a frank cynicism she'd be unwise to ignore...?

'There will be lots of people at the *grand bal*, you say?' Marianne added in a harder voice, 'I wouldn't be so sure. By the time Tante Mirrie has finished with the good villagers of St-Pierre-de-Mordin, I should be surprised if more than ten people turn up, Emily!'

'Please come,' Emily persisted softly. 'I'd love to see you all again...'

Another exclamation of disgust heralded the crash of Marianne's receiver and the uncompromising drone of the dialling tone. Slowly Emily replaced her end and stared helplessly at the black telephone on her desk for a long time before switching her attention back to her word processor.

She was poring over the filing cabinet when Greg Vernon sauntered in. He looked dusty and tousled, clad only in khaki shorts, revealing a sun-bronzed chest and quite respectable pectoral muscles. He came to sit on the edge of her desk, and she felt his hazel eyes roaming over her figure in her neat navy checked cotton shirtwaister.

'Hello, gorgeous! I'm just off for a long, cold beer in the village. Want to come?'

'Sorry. I'm busy,' she said coolly, pushing past him to get back to her chair. 'And I seem to recall

Christian Malraux throwing you out of here and telling you not to come back?'

'I'm working for the village carpenter, not the Mighty Malraux,' Greg drawled unrepentantly. 'Besides, you can't order me around like a lackey. I'm a mature student, sweetheart.' He grinned good-humouredly. 'I may be bumming round Europe for the summer, but back home I'm doing a sociology degree. Brains as well as brawn, like you!'

The telephone rang. With a withering look at Greg, she lifted the receiver. Christian's deep voice brought her bolt upright in her chair. She'd been thinking about him with such fierce, buried longing, she wondered if she'd conjured him up via some telepathic communication.

'Emily? Is everything all right?'

'Yes—er—no!' Involuntarily, she dragged her fingers through her dishevelled curls, wiped her shaking hand over her face. A ridiculous mixture of excitement and pleasure, apprehension and resentment filled her at the sound of his voice, and she tried severely to control her breathless confusion. Her heart was jumping madly.

'Come on, Emily, let's go and have that drink, sweetheart,' Greg said loudly, with a grin, coming behind her chair to slide his arms round her waist and nuzzle her neck. With a muffled shriek she stood up, pushing him furiously away.

'Who the hell is that?' Christian's clipped query sounded cold as steel.

'Greg ... he's helping to prepare for the *grand bal*,' she said hurriedly, aiming an accurate backward kick at Greg's shin and feeling it connect with a stab of triumph. Greg's jokey, mock-anguished protest was an added goad.

'I'll bet he is.' Christian was bitingly sardonic. 'Just remember I'm paying you to type letters and make phone calls, not waste time flirting in the office or going for drinks during working hours. Do I make myself clear, Emily?'

Rigid with a sudden wave of fury, she flashed back softly, 'Not entirely, no! I was under the impression my duties round here far exceeded typing and telephone calls, Monsieur Malraux!'

'Whatever gave you that idea, Mademoiselle Gainsborough?'

The icy drawl cut her to the core.

'*Christian* . . . ?' Infuriated, she heard the line click and go dead. The second person to hang up on her in the space of an hour. Slamming the receiver down with such violence that it bounced back off again, she turned her full anger on Greg, who was playfully backing away to the door, hands up in mock surrender.

'Sorry, did I stir things up?'

'Get out of here,' she flung at him shakily. 'And stay out of my way, please?'

'Whatever you say, Emily.' He swaggered out, and she watched as he emerged into the sunlit courtyard and made a beeline for Lisette, who was drinking cola out of a can and gesturing to the workmen in an airy, superior fashion. Greg Vernon was an irritating pain in the neck, Emily judged wearily, sinking back into her chair. But

Christian was impossible—arrogant, insufferably egotistical ...

And he hadn't even said when he'd be back.

When the workmen had finished for the night Lisette announced grudgingly that there was a *salade Niçoise*, grilled pork and pasta for supper later, then went off with Greg to the village. It was a hot, airless evening. After a long, cool shower and hair-wash, Emily spent an hour in her room, wrapped in a large towel, writing postcards to all her friends, and to her parents and Ben. She kept the messages brief. She even cheated by repeating the same words on several of them. Concentration eluded her. She couldn't stop thinking about Christian, about the painful shambles of their relationship. And about the dance on Saturday night. And about Mathieu Colbert, and Marianne and the rest of the family...

Restless and hungry, she shrugged on white canvas jeans and a sleeveless pink checked blouse and made her way down to the big, old-fashioned kitchen, with its tall cream-painted Georgian cupboards and massive pine table, and checked the fridge. It was efficiently full of food. For old Uncle Thierry Lisette had cooked a full lunch every day of the week—for her employer and for fellow château workers. The French girl was a superb cook.

Emily had the impression that, since Christian had come to take charge, Lisette might have been feeling rather bored and redundant. Christian was more erratic in his needs. He was restless, had

no desire to settle into a cosy routine at the
château. He frequently went to restaurants for
meals; he was often away. The estate workers ate
at the *relais routier* in the village, or brought a
sandwich to eat in the walled gardens. When
Christian was here and wanted to eat at the
château, or even when he wasn't here, Emily felt
awkward being served meals by Lisette. It wasn't
an easy problem to overcome. She would have
liked to strike up a friendship with the other girl.
But they were at daggers drawn, and things
seemed set to stay that way. Was it because Lisette
saw Emily as a rival for Christian's attentions?
Her heart sank as she thought about the scene
she'd witnessed... Lisette, coming out of
Christian's apartment, looking sensuously
dishevelled, with that sly satisfaction in her
eyes...

With no sign of Lisette returning, Emily extracted a chop from the fridge, slicked butter and
garlic slivers over it, and put it under the grill.
She filled a pan with salted water to boil the fine-
cut macaroni which Lisette had nominated as the
accompaniment. She was just laying a place for
herself at the kitchen table, and dishing out some
of the salad, when there was a scrunch of tyres
on gravel outside. Emily's heart jolted in her
chest. She recognised those tyres. Christian was
back.

He appeared in the kitchen doorway a moment
later, pausing to survey the scene in sardonic
silence. In faded, button-fly Levis, loose white
T-shirt and suede ankle boots, he looked tough

and casual, and devastatingly attractive. Emily had to fight down a foolish rush of pleasure at the sight of him.

'Hello...' Warily she kept her voice cool and polite.

'I was drawn by the smell of cooking,' he murmured, deadpan. 'Is there enough for two?'

'Yes... of course.' Flustered but determined not to show it, she calmly set about adding another chop to the grill, measured out more pasta. 'Although I'm not sure you pay me to cook you meals in the evenings, Monsieur Malraux.'

'I'm not quite sure what I'm paying you for at the moment,' he countered flatly, dropping into a chair at the table. He directed a hard gaze at her, resting his elbows on the scrubbed pine with an air of fatigue which tore at her heart. 'Where's your English lover-boy? I'd have thought you'd be cooking a cosy meal for the two of you this evening?'

'Well, I would be, of course!' she retorted. 'But I was tired after all the wild *orgies* I've been indulging in since you went to Paris. So, to vary things, Greg's out with your alternative bedmate, Lisette.'

However hard she strived for flippant sarcasm, she was unable to disguise the bitterness in her voice.

'Let's at least get one thing straightened out,' Christian murmured laconically, his eyes chips of blue ice between narrowed black lashes. 'I am not sleeping with Lisette. And I have no desire to sleep with Lisette.'

'Then what was she doing in your apartment that evening? When I got back from Saintes?'

There was an infinitesimal pause, before Christian said drily, 'I didn't say that Lisette had no desire to sleep with me.'

Emily felt herself go hot all over. 'So you're saying she flung herself at you in a flurry of unrequited passion?'

Christian's eyebrow tilted wryly at her accusing tone. 'Isn't that more or less your story over Greg Vernon?'

She couldn't bear the contemptuous glitter in his gaze. He didn't believe her innocence over her association with Greg. Emily had her pride. She wasn't going to beg him to believe her...

There was an ominous sizzling from the grill. Glad of the diversion, she gave the chops elaborate concentration as she flipped them over, added more butter and garlic, lowered the heat. The rich, savoury aroma wafted around the kitchen. Dishing the main course up to keep warm, she fetched the bowl of *salade Niçoise* and a fresh baguette, and placed another setting at the table.

'How was Paris?' she enquired sweetly, determined to defuse the mounting tension.

'Paris was...' Christian raked his hands wearily over his face and through his thick dark hair, then leaned back in his chair '...cathartic.'

'Oh?' She took another quick look in the fridge, and discovered a bottle of white wine, half full. She placed it on the table, with napkins and glasses. 'How do you mean, exactly?'

'Marc is going to live. He's going to be fine. I'd had nightmares of him being crippled for life, like Mathieu Colbert. Another near-miss on my conscience. "There, but for the grace of God"? Some of my superstitions were put to rest, maybe.' Christian poured wine into both glasses and took a hefty gulp from his. The look he levelled at her when he put his glass down made her pulses jump and drum in apprehension.

'Superstitions?' she echoed faintly. 'Christian, what are you talking about?'

'The feeling that maybe I'm...cursed by the gods. That I bring people bad luck, Emily.' The deep, husky voice was casual, cynical, almost bored. But there was something in his eyes which touched her soul.

She stared at him in silence. The tension was so thick that it was like a tangible layer between them. She dropped her knife and fork on to her plate, half drowning in the brilliant black-fringed blue of his eyes.

'That's not true. I know it isn't. Christian, explain what you mean. Please. Talk to me,' she whispered, with a shiver of intense yearning which took her by surprise. 'Please?'

'About what?' Christian took a mouthful of salad and a piece of bread, his dark blue gaze unfathomable.

'About Mathieu? And Marie-Claire? Isn't that what this is all about?'

'The superstitions go back further than that,' he grinned bleakly, self-mockingly. 'Right back to my parents' death. I always had a strange feeling about them dying and not me.'

'Why?'

He shrugged. 'No logical reason. It wasn't until the episode with the Colbert family that I even noticed the feeling, to be honest...'

'Christian...' Emily speared a black olive with her fork and gazed at his dark face uncomprehendingly. The evening light outside was fading. There were shadows forming in the corners of the old kitchen. 'You told me your parents died in a hotel fire in India, when you were very young?'

'They did.'

'Then what in heaven's name could have given you that...that *ridiculous* superstitious feeling?'

'At the time, nothing. It wasn't until Marie-Claire tried to kill herself, and then the car-crash with Mathieu, when I was a grown man, and thought I knew better.' His smile was humourless, deepening the sardonic grooves on either side of his mouth. He toyed with his salad then pushed it away. 'Shall I tell you when I really began to speculate on angry gods, or ancient curses, Emily? When I met you. The coincidence is too ironic, don't you agree? Of all the people in the world I could care about, of all the females I could find deeply attractive, she turns out to be an old friend of my sworn enemies, the Colberts? As final retribution it's quite neat, don't you think?'

Had he said he found her deeply attractive? Had he just said he could care about her? Emily

was trembling inside. An urgent need to get closer
to him again, to somehow bridge this cold,
painful gulf between them, overrode pride, anger
and caution.

'Christian...' Her voice cracked, and she
caught her breath, and forged on. 'You seem to
have this thing with the Colberts blown out of
all proportion in your head. Even if Marianne's
version of what happened is true in every bitter
detail, it doesn't make you a monster! You...you
seem to be so...so eaten up with guilt, or bitterness, or both...the moment you knew that
Marianne had told me her side of the story, you
blocked me out...'

'Did I?' There was wry humour somewhere,
shuttered inside his expression. 'I seem to recall
hauling you into bed..'

'*Mentally* blocked me out,' she amended unsteadily, searching his hard face with wide, perplexed brown eyes. Her stomach was cramped
into knots of emotion and apprehension, 'Physically, sex seems to be your answer to
everything...!'

'It's uncomplicated,' he pointed out, his mouth
twisting as he added lightly, 'At least, it can be...'

'So is the truth,' she said urgently, passion
giving emphasis to her words. 'So is
having...having *faith* in yourself, facing up to
mistakes and...and *forgiving* yourself! If I have
faith in you, why can't you have faith in
yourself?'

'Why should you have faith in me?' he queried
bluntly. The scar on his cheek looked more jagged

than ever, as he turned to intently study her flushed face, 'What in sweet hell do you know about me, Emily?'

'Not a great deal, maybe,' she returned quietly, desperation creeping into her voice. 'But I do know that I feel . . . close to you. That I've felt close to you from the first moment we met. In a way I can't explain. Don't ask me to. It's not fair. I can't answer you . . .'

'*Bon sang*, Emily . . .' He shook his head with abrupt impatience, grim humour glinting in his eyes, 'Not only do I get the physical come-on, I get the mystical "karma" line, too?'

The colour flooded her face, then abruptly receded, leaving her chalk-white. 'That's a foul thing to say!'

'*Je m'excuse*, Emily.' He reached to touch her hand, sending tremors of electricity through her system. She stood up, trembling, and fetched the pork and pasta, suddenly conscious that the darkness was invading the room. Christian had observed it too. Ignoring the light switch, he fetched a candle, found matches. The wavering halo of light threw ghostly shadows across the room, then strengthened into a steady golden glow as they sat down again to eat the pork Emily had cooked.

'There. A romantic setting for this travesty of domesticity,' he taunted. 'This is good,' he added, spearing a tender piece of pork. 'You can cook too? As well as your many other talents?'

'Passably well . . .' The food tasted like sawdust in her tight throat. Why was he being so foul?

Self-defence? Or did he genuinely believe she was enjoying a spot of casual sex with Greg? That, having been initiated into sensual pleasures, she'd developed an insatiable taste for variety?

'My... my mother is a very keen cook.' She forced herself to speak calmly. 'Creating mouth-watering, elegant meals and inviting friends round to join her is one of her main hobbies...'

'She sounds worth meeting.'

'You must come home and meet her. I'd love that...' Emily spoke without thinking, then caught her lower lip between her teeth.

'*Merci*, Emily.' Christian's tone was wry, but she thought she detected a faint gleam of tenderness in his eyes as he watched her embarrassment. Then her heart contracted painfully when he added, 'But I doubt if I fit the type to be taken home to meet your mother. A man you believe capable of casually sleeping with two women at the same time, and worst of all a man who has committed crimes against a family you have known since you were a child?'

'Committed crimes?' she echoed, with a lurch of angry misery. 'A broken engagement, and a car accident? You're *paranoid* about what happened with the Colberts, aren't you?'

He shrugged again, his own anger evident in the tense set of his jaw.

'I thought I'd forgotten it all, put it all behind me. Coming back has triggered it off again. I was engaged to Marie-Claire. When I broke it off, she took an overdose of aspirin and almost died. Mathieu was deeply upset. There was an angry scene one night. We crashed, in my car, and he was critically injured. As far as the Colberts were concerned, it was a double betrayal...'

'And as far as you're concerned it's meant never risking getting close to anyone again?'

'Perhaps...' Christian's eyes hardened on Emily's searching gaze. 'In my experience, it is very rarely worth the effort.'

The cruelty of his words was like a physical slap in the face. White-faced, feeling subtly humiliated, she stared down at her clenched hands in her lap.

'You're right,' she managed with bitter humour. 'I see now how... how right you were when you gave me that cynical, world-weary warning of yours that first night! But if risking involvement with someone isn't worth the effort, settling your score with the Colberts must be. I've invited them all here, to the *grand bal*, on Saturday night...'

Christian was motionless. He stayed still and silent for so long, she imagined he could have turned to stone.

'Are you completely mad?' he queried at last. The softness in his tone was far more alarming and ominous than direct anger.

She swallowed convulsively, gave a shaky laugh. 'That's exactly what Marianne said....'

'Precisely.' Christian's hard mouth twisted, 'They will not come, Emily. Not all the demons in hell would drag the Colberts here to Château de Mordin. In fact, now that the local black sheep has returned, there must be a large question mark over whether most of the village will boycott the event!'

'That's crazy, and you know it! Whatever angry feelings the Colberts have, to the rest of the world you were all victims of circumstance! Stop feeling guilty! It's self-destructive, Christian! You'll go mad, locking all this bitterness and self-recrimination inside yourself!'

'You count a diploma in psychology among your qualifications?'

She stood up, unable to face any more of his cynical mockery.

'Excuse me. I'm tired. I'll go to bed...'

'Alone?' Christian had stood up, too. The lidded blue gaze was scathingly bleak as he scanned her flushed face. 'Would it be more convenient to move back into the other wing of the château now, Emily? To make yourself more accessible to night visitors?'

A haze of fury engulfed her. Blindly she swung her hand at him, catching him hard on the cheek with her palm. Almost instantly, her arm was imprisoned in a vice-like grip which brought tears of pain to her eyes.

'You're detestable! I hate you!'

'Healthier than all this faith and trust,' he mocked ruthlessly, dragging her into his arms and holding her there, hard against him. 'Maybe you're seeing me as I really am at last?'

'Maybe I am!' She half-sobbed the words as she writhed to free herself, to no avail. 'You have a low, despicable mind! And you're a hypocrite!

You expect me to believe you're not involved with Lisette, but you're determined to believe the worst of me, on the strength of some flimsy circumstantial evidence ... !'

'I'm just a naturally suspicious male.' He gave a short, humourless laugh. 'I could go after Greg Vernon and beat his goddamned brains out, but I don't think I'll bother. You're pretty good at doing your own fighting, aren't you, Emily?'

'That depends on my opponent,' she whispered painfully, rubbing her arm where his fingers had bruised the soft flesh. 'And it depends whether it's worth the effort!'

'You took the words right out of my mouth,' he sneered softly. 'Our brief involvement has been a departure from my normal caution, Emily. All it has done is confirm what I knew all along...'

White and shaking, she summoned all her strength to move as he abruptly released her. Blinking back hot tears, she stared into his harsh face.

'I don't know what you're so... afraid of! I'm not going to try and trap you into a commitment you don't want! You don't have to drag what we had into the mud, just to extricate yourself from me! Surely you don't have to convince yourself I'm sleeping with Greg Vernon just to give yourself some justification for... for *dumping* me! Just go right ahead! But do it honestly! Don't flatter yourself I won't get over it!'

Turning away quickly to hide the tell-tale stinging in her eyes, she hugged her arms around herself, swallowed the huge choked lump of emotion in her throat. She wanted to escape, she wanted to run up to her room, but her knees felt so weak that she couldn't move. Instead, she willed him to go away. Willed him to go out of the kitchen, and leave her to break down and cry.

'Emily...'

The deep voice held a thicker note of emotion, and she caught her breath in panic.

'Please leave me alone...' she whispered raggedly. 'Go away, Christian... just go away.'

It was a bitter-sweet relief when, after a short, tense silence, the door clicked decisively, angrily shut behind her, and she turned her head and realised through the blur of tears that he had gone.

CHAPTER EIGHT

'EMILY? Wake up...'

She blinked in the early morning sunlight and turned her head on the pillow. Christian stood there with a breakfast tray, his expression unreadable as he gazed down at her. Dishevelled and flustered, she blinked and struggled to sit up.

'What...what are you doing in here?'

'Marvelling at how deeply you sleep,' he murmured drily, glancing at his watch. Alarmed, she swivelled her head to look at the clock by the bed, and then gasped in dismay.

'Oh! I've overslept. I'm sorry...I...'

'Had a bad night?' Christian supplied grimly, drawing up a chair and setting the tray on her lap. His eyes moved briefly over the tender jut of her breasts through her thin white cotton nightshirt, and she tensed. There was coffee on the tray, and warm croissants. And fresh orange juice. The aromas drifted up, arousing her tastebuds despite her tension.

'I am the one to say sorry,' he added, his deep voice lacking expression. 'I came back from Paris last night in a black mood, Emily. It was not fair to inflict my blackness on you.'

'So instead you decided to inflict pity on me this morning?' she hazarded, with bitter self-mockery. 'There's no need. I did a lot of thinking last night. This...this mess is all my fault. You said it would be a very bad idea for us to...to get involved! I shouldn't have let my silly...infatuation show in the first place. Then things wouldn't have got so...heavy...'

Christian said nothing for a long time. When she turned to look at him, there was an unfathomable light in his eyes, disturbing, cruelly unsettling to her composure. In khaki bermudas exposing long muscular legs, and a faded denim shirt, he somehow managed to look so devastatingly attractive that her stomach went into meltdown all over again. With angry impatience she raked shaky fingers through her blonde curls, dreading how she must look. She'd cried a lot of bitter tears into her pillow last night. Her eyes still felt puffy and sore.

'I haven't come to inflict pity on you, as you put it,' he said at last, 'but I feel...responsible. I had no right to take advantage of a young girl in my employ, Emily. I should have been more careful. I should have had more self-control...'

'I see...' Her voice was annoyingly croaky as she sought to control her feelings. 'Could you please go away now? I'll be down in the office in half an hour...'

A wry smile twisted his mouth. Pulling up a chair, he shook his head slowly.

'Since you've overslept so long, I've given up on office work,' he announced. 'I've come to take you out for the day...'

She stared at him in resentful disbelief. 'I'd rather work, thanks all the same.'

'The good thing about being the boss is you get to make the rules. No work today. So eat your breakfast, and pack your beach-bag.'

'My beach-bag?' She felt colour creeping into her cheeks at the cool arrogance of his orders. 'Christian, what makes you think I'd want to go to the beach with you today?'

'What makes you think you have any choice in the matter, *ma mignonne*?'

'What do you *want* from me?' she burst out, goaded into fury. 'Do you want me to grovel, do you want to gloat...?'

'I want to lighten things up between us. I said things last night in the heat of the moment,' Christian said with quiet determination, 'things I certainly never meant to say. And I'd like to know how you feel...'

'*Angry*! That's how I feel! And betrayed...'

'How have I betrayed you?' His voice was quiet, intense, but expressionless. Her heart was thumping. 'Tell me, Emily? How? Through not being the person you'd naïvely expected?'

'You've betrayed me by not trusting me! By believing I could switch on to someone else, so soon after sharing what I shared with you! And don't call me naïve! I understand a lot more about you than you think!'

'Oh? Enlighten me.'

'You're...you're bitter and twisted about things that went wrong in your life, things in the past. You've let this negative attitude colour everything you do. You've let it block any chance of happiness...'

Christian's expression was shuttered. 'And you have experienced nothing in your life to make you wary of happiness, Emily?'

'No, I don't think so! But there's nothing particularly clever about being bitter and miserable, is there?'

Christian shook his head slowly, searching her angry face, a faint glimmer of a smile in his eyes.

'No. There is not. And tell me, Emily, do you have the fail-safe recipe for my happiness?'

A rush of heat surged and receded, leaving her feeling weak and shaky.

'No... of course not!' She wished her voice didn't sound so husky. 'That's something that... that has to come from inside you...'

He reached across, took the tray and put it down on the table by the bed. Then, without warning, he moved to put his arms round her, sliding his hands around her back, his fingers smoothing the sleep-warm silkiness of her skin at the sleeveless armholes of her nightshift. An involuntary shudder went through her. With a soft, thick noise in his throat Christian imperceptibly tightened his hold on her, pulling her hard into his arms. Dizzying sensations swamped her. Her breasts were crushed against his chest, and she felt branded by the heat from his body. Her intellect was fighting his arrogance, his shameless show of male strength, but her stomach was melting, hollow with longing.

'You smell of musk and flowers,' he growled hoarsely, the mocking amusement in his eyes darkening into a now familiar glint which wrecked her composure. 'I don't know about happiness coming from inside me . . . I want to be inside you, Emily, right now . . .'

With the boldly outrageous words he moved to lie beside her on the bed, deflecting her wild punches of defence, outlining the high jut of her breasts until the nipples sprang harder into his hand, then pushing the covers back and running a predatory palm down her slender thighs.

'Stop this . . . oh, Christian, please . . . !'

'Please? Are you begging me to stop, or begging me to remind you of what it was like between us, my sexy little Emily?'

The husky murmur came as he moved his fingers higher, rumpling the edge of the nightshift to her hips, and hungrily slipping his fingers between her legs. She cried out, tensing and arching in mingled anger and desire as he sought and found the warm, moist secrets there, boldly investigating until she was trembling convulsively beneath his skilful caresses.

Fighting was no use. It made things worse. He covered her mouth in a deep, searching kiss, then rolled so that she was flattened against his full length, crushing her buttocks with his hand, so that she was moulded intimately against his hips. It was impossible to ignore the hard thrust of his desire against her softness. She'd never felt more vulnerable, more agonised and confused...

'Christian, for pity's sake...' It was a hot, anguished whisper.

'I want to be oceans deep inside you, *ma mignonne*,' he teased implacably, his voice thick with emotion, lifting his head away to look into her flushed face. The predatory hunger in his eyes deepened the blue to rich, dark cobalt, shadowed with black. 'So deep, you'll never be able to forget how it feels when I take possession of you...'

'Don't...*don't*!' It was a breathless hiss of protest. Hectic flags of colour stained her cheeks. By an immense exercise of will-power she managed to thrust herself partially free, breathing jerkily as she glared into the dark, mocking face. She was trembling with fury. 'This is all a game to you, isn't it? On one level—a physical level! I can't believe I could have been so foolish as to let my...my heart rule my head! I can't believe I could have wanted you to be my first lover...!'

'Why?' he countered softly. 'We were attracted...sexually. We still are. Be honest. Practise what you preach. It was good between us. What has changed? Why expect sexual desire to die just because you have revised your opinion of my character, Emily?'

'Will you stop talking as if I think badly of your character?' she flung at him huskily.

'But you think I took advantage of your day off in Saintes to make love to Lisette?' He was softly persistent.

'OK, if you say you didn't, I believe you! But you believe I'm capable of sleeping with *Greg Vernon*!' she exploded, goaded beyond caution. 'If you love someone, you don't instantly believe the worst of them! Trust and faith are everything—without them there's no point in anything else...' She was dimly aware of an illogical streak in this assertion, but she felt too confused to rectify it.

Christian had become motionless. He didn't move a muscle as he intently searched her face.

'If you *love* someone, Emily?' he echoed finally. The deep voice held a brutal taunt. 'I assume we are talking hypothetically now?'

'Yes! What else?' she spat back, thrusting an unsteady hand to force him even further away from her. 'You don't imagine I was talking about *you*?' Panic gave a sharp edge to her voice as she ploughed on, 'Love takes time to grow, doesn't it? It doesn't happen overnight. You can't love someone you don't even know! You can't love someone who won't talk, who won't share, who can't lift himself out of the... the *base* instincts and see there's more to relationships than sex! I don't love you! I *hate* you!'

'Emily...' The deep voice held wry regret, but something else too, something which caught at her heart. 'Be fair. You accused me of wanting nothing but sex. But when I offer to take you out for the day, you complain.'

She shivered as he caressed the full length of her body in one last, possessive sweep, then firmly twisted her round so that her feet were on the floor.

'See? Just to prove once again that I can rise above the base instincts,' he taunted softly, the dark dilation of his pupils betraying his desire, 'So loosen up, *chérie*. We both went into this relationship knowing the pitfalls. Let's see if we can part friends?'

Emily stared at him, devastated, unable to say a word.

Part friends? She could hardly assimilate his meaning. And then it sank in with painful finality. He was telling her it was over. He was being logical, adult, and terrifyingly practical. It had all become too complicated. He'd made it clear from the start that he didn't specialise in emotional complications.

But until now she had been ashamed to admit to herself that there'd lingered some stubborn, illogical streak of romanticism, or optimism. She'd secretly cherished a faint hope. Christian's frank, blunt statement seemed to hit her straight in the stomach, sadistically cruel and distressing after he'd aroused her to such a humiliating peak of desire...

She chewed her lower lip distractedly and her breath left her in a rush. The dark pit of bleak unhappiness opening before her was more frightening than anything she'd faced in her life...

Sickly, she found herself nodding, shrugging calmly.

'So you want to take me out for the day to salve a guilty conscience? You're right, let's be civilised about this. Would you mind starting by giving me some privacy while I get dressed, *this* time?'

'*Bien sûr*, Emily.' His deep voice was a velvety caress which tore at her heart. With an infuriatingly triumphant smile, he picked up the tray and replaced it on her knees. '*A toute à l'heure*. See you later. Don't forget your breakfast...'

Forty minutes later, numb inside and out, she sat beside him as they headed for the coast. The sea was only twenty kilometres away. The powerful Mercedes purred along the country road, bisecting the fields of sunflowers and the endless vineyards with effortless precision. Emily, arms folded in stiff defence, glared sightlessly out of the windscreen, conscious only of the breeze lifting her hair and cooling her hot face as they drove.

'You know,' she managed at last, 'it seems to be your strongest character trait—having a guilty conscience! Would you agree?'

'I'm no great analyst of my own character.'

'What a pity. Because I think you'd find it makes fascinating analysis. You feel guilty for "taking advantage" of me, as you put it,' she bit out with a shaky laugh, 'and at the same time you are eaten up by guilt because of what happened with the Colberts five years ago. You even harbour guilty feelings from... from your early childhood! You feel guilty because your parents died and you lived! You feel guilty because a journalist colleague is injured taking on one of your assignments. You feel guilty about *living*! You're afraid you make other people unhappy just by breathing!'

'If you say so.' Christian's sardonic profile was harshly uncompromising. If her words had dented his defences, he gave no indication.

They were pulling off the road on to a thickly wooded track. Dense pine trees dappled the hot sunshine, scenting the air with resin. Braking sharply, he halted the car and turned to catch Emily's face in his hands, bending his dark head abruptly to kiss her, full and hard, on the mouth. When he lifted his head, and saw the dazed look in her eyes, he gave a short laugh.

'I've certainly made you unhappy, Emily,' he stated, bleakly mocking. 'In just a short space of time I have succeeded in turning a bright, bouncy little extrovert into a tearful waif! What would your parents, your brother think if they could see the state you are in?'

'You are so arrogant, you try to take the credit for everything,' she murmured with an attempt at sarcastic humour, then gave a muffled cry as he kissed the words back into her mouth, deepened the embrace until the taste and smell and feel of him was all that existed for the moment.

It took all her will-power not to twist her hands round his neck, run her fingers into the dark spring of his hair, cling to him tightly to try to heal this bitter gulf between them...

'We'd better drive on,' he said thickly, a little while later, lifting his head and gazing down into her bemused, flushed face, his eyes dark with desire. 'We could get arrested for doing what I feel like doing right now...'

'Oh, Christian...!' She glared at him in fierce resentment. 'I *wish* I'd never met you!'

'*Attention*, Emily,' His smile was a bitter twist of the mouth. 'Be careful. My ego is fatally damaged already...'

She stared silently into his lidded eyes, wide brown locked with brilliant blue. Crickets were shrilling in the pine woods. The high, monotonous whine seemed to suspend animation. Nothing moved in the heat. Somewhere in the distance, she could hear the crash of the Atlantic.

Then, with a soft curse, Christian pulled back from her and started the engine again. Tears stung her eyes and she blinked them back furiously. They drove over a bumpy track, finishing up at some heavy wooden gates. A mossy sign announced that it was private land. In slight confusion, Emily watched while Christian got out, opened the gates, then drove through them. A rather gothic-style house, three-storeyed and high-gabled, emerged through a dense copse of Corsican pine. A wide, empty golden crescent of sand stretched beyond it, blending into a sparkling turquoise sea. Moderately sized waves crashed playfully at the edge.

'What's this place?' she managed to ask, scrubbing her eyes impatiently and blowing her nose, 'I thought we were going to the beach.'

'And here you have one. My beach.' He intercepted her blank look, and added calmly, 'I have owned this house for years. Don't look so worried. A local couple come in three times a week to clean and maintain it. It will not be damp and spider-infested...'

It wasn't. The house was beautiful, cool and airy. When its shutters were folded back, its interior walls proved to be white-painted, rustic-style. There was lots of solid dark oak furniture, flagstoned floors, jewel-bright Indian rugs. Outside there was a big crazy-paved terrace, shaded by a wooden pergola, with a tangle of roses, clematis and numerous other climbing plants making an archway on to a lawn, and then to the beach. Wild yellow broom grew everywhere. Its sweet perfume blended with the heady aroma of pine needles, and the salty tang of the hot sand and the sea. The combination scented the air so heavily that it was like breathing incense.

'*Et voilà*, a picnic.' Christian produced an enormous wicker hamper, like a magician. It had been put in the cool green kitchen, ready for them. 'I rang ahead, early this morning,' he explained, seeing her bewilderment. 'The couple who look after the house have been busy...'

Emily glanced at the contents of the hamper, shaking her head disbelievingly. The bitter-sweet experience of being here with him, so outwardly close and so inwardly estranged, was making her feel slightly light-headed.

'Fresh *langoustines*. Roast chicken. Ripe peaches. Strawberries. The bread smells wonderful. You were so confident I'd come?'

'If you'd knocked me out cold with a right hook and roared off to the airport, I'd probably have come by myself.' He grinned lazily. 'I'd still have reached the stage where I needed to unwind...'

She shrugged, unwilling to unwind completely and laugh with him. 'So what do we do now?'

'Now? We go wind-surfing...'

'You're joking! I've never wind-surfed in my life...'

'In this part of France, *tout le monde* wind-surfs. I'll teach you.'

Emily was getting to know Christian well enough by now to realise she'd get nowhere arguing. And suddenly from the pit of black misery crept a small tingling sense of well-being as she scanned the blue sky, the endless pine woods, the golden sand, the softly breaking Atlantic rollers.

'OK.' She shrugged, with a ghost of her old smile dimpling her cheek. 'But you're a brave man.'

'You'll be a natural,' he assured her, eyeing her slender but well-muscled body beneath her white shorts and jade T-shirt.

Two hours later, exultant as she managed to sail upright for ten yards, she crashed once more into the water and emerged spluttering and swearing under her breath in a most unladylike manner, tugging impatiently on the rope which connected her to the sailboard.

'You're doing well!' Christian called across. He was skimming across the sparkling blue water with awesome speed and dexterity. She shot him a malevolent look.

'I think I'm getting the hang of it, if you'd just stop being so damn patronising!' she yelled defiantly.

'It's exhilarating, isn't it?' he grinned, closing the gap between them and watching her attempts to climb back on board with a commendably deadpan expression. 'Are you always so fiercely defensive when you're being taught something new?'

'Put it down to twenty-two years' merciless teasing from an older brother!' She gritted her teeth, every inch of muscle in her body taut with the effort of succeeding. She was up on her feet, perilously wobbly, but she'd regained her balance. Legs braced, she began the slow, exhausting process of hauling up the sail. Her jade bikini was lamentably designed for water-sports. With each stretch of her slender limbs it slipped or rode up or played some other unfair trick to shake her poise under that narrowed, amused blue gaze.

'Bravo!' Christian admired, grinning even more broadly as she lost her balance again and crashed back overboard. Fortunately, Emily's momentary lapse into gutter language was smothered beneath the Atlantic. When she swam to the surface she had herself firmly in hand.

'Time for lunch,' he called, swivelling his sail skilfully into the wind and skimming fast towards the shore. 'We'll put in some more practice later.'

'If there's one thing I can't stand, it's a show-off!' she announced, with a rueful laugh, emerging in the shallows to haul her board out of the water.

'So I gathered.' Christian's glance was teasing as they regained the terrace, and he went to fetch the hamper from its cool storage place. 'Does your big brother have any idea of how he's shaped your personality, Emily?'

'Probably not,' she admitted lightly, collapsing on to a padded garden chair and adjusting the halter strap of her bikini, 'Anyway, you're exaggerating slightly! I only said he teased me. All brothers do that.'

Ravening hunger had gripped her after the exertion and the cool, bracing sea-water. She foraged in the hamper, found a juicy chicken portion and a hunk of fresh baguette. Christian watched her through lidded eyes as he extracted a bottle of white wine and proceeded to open it.

'You look like a starving sea-nymph,' he murmured, handing her a glass of wine, 'water dripping down your face, falling on your food as if it might be your last meal...'

A tinge of colour warmed her face. She put the half-eaten chicken down, glancing up at him through her lashes.

'Don't stop,' he amended lazily, taking a mouthful of his wine, 'You look adorable. I have never spent as much time in a girl's company and discovered that, far from getting severely on my nerves, I like all her habits and mannerisms...'

'Christian, for heaven's sake...'

'Right down to your entertaining methods of self-defence, your refreshingly boyish vocabulary of rude words when you lose your temper with yourself, your courage and determination, and your uninhibited appetite for food...'

'Really?' she countered, acidly, trying to suppress the sudden secret pounding of her heart under that laid-back stare. 'And you're going to miss all these endearing little mannerisms of mine when I'm gone?'

'*Sans doute*, Emily. Without a doubt. But you have your future mapped out, *n'est-ce pas*?'

Speechless, she continued to eat. But now the food had lost some of its tempting succulence.

'Have I offended you?' he probed softly. He was peeling an enormous *langoustine* with a speed and skill only a Frenchman could possess. Reluctantly, Emily stared at him, allowed herself to appreciate the glorious sight of his dark hair-roughened body in the minuscule black swimming-trunks, the nonchalant lack of inhibition as he sprawled in his chair, rangy and muscular and overpoweringly masculine. He glanced up, caught her clouded expression, and added unexpectedly, 'Could it be that you no longer *want* to follow your career plans?'

'What I decide to do with my life is really none of your business, Christian.'

'You have spent your life determined to prove yourself as ambitious and reliable as your brother,' he mused, ignoring her shaky snub. 'You have avoided the unsettling world of emotional . . . liaisons. You have been haunted by an irrational fear of ending up a contented little housewife, without ambition or power, like your mother.'

'You may be right. I've a feeling I told you all this myself! And there's nothing wrong in any of those things. What exactly are you driving at?'

He put the *langoustine* in his mouth and ate it with unconcerned relish before he answered.

'I am trying to make sense of what happened between us.'

From an angry, wide-eyed glare Emily dropped her eyes to her plate again. 'In the cool light of day?' she suggested, with a short laugh. 'I . . . we were sexually attracted to each other. I'd say that sums it up,' she said stiffly. 'I'm twenty-two. Face it, it had to happen to me some time! It just happened to be . . . you.'

'And I am thirty. It has already happened to me many times, Emily.'

Trembling inwardly, she put her plate down with elaborate care on the table, and took a strawberry from the bowl. Picking carefully at the leafy green hull, she slowly bit into the sweet fruit.

'As if I didn't know,' she said at last, avoiding his eyes. 'You don't exactly come over as inexperienced, Christian! There's really no need to *boast*!'

'It was not intended to be a boast, Emily.' He sounded patient, thoughtful. 'Although sexual attraction has taken many... interesting guises in my life so far, it has never before involved so many disturbing emotions...'

She turned to look at him, then, a frown beginning to crease between her eyebrows. 'You were engaged to marry someone, remember?' she pointed out flatly. 'Are you trying to tell me no emotions were involved in *that* relationship?'

'You are deliberately misunderstanding.' There was a harder edge to his voice now. 'For men, there is often a difference between instant sexual desire and feelings of a more... durable kind.'

'Oh, *I* see! You mean girls who are too eager for sex are *not* the kind of women who make good wives? There's a kind of woman you marry and raise children with, and a kind you obtain wild nights of passion with, outside marriage? Is that the way you do things round here? Quaint double standards?'

'*Arrête*, Emily! Stop!' She'd succeeded in provoking him. Anger smoked ominously in the

narrowed blue gaze as he raked her hot face.
'Stop twisting my meaning. *Bon sang*! I had
thought we could talk rationally today—relax,
and have a civilised conversation!'

'Maybe we don't have a *civilised* relationship?'

'Maybe we don't.'

There was a long silence. Tense with confused
anger and misery, Emily stared out to sea. A big
tanker was visible on the horizon, probably
heading for Bordeaux. The sun glinted off the
rippling waves, dazzling her. Finally, as the
silence threatened to spin out indefinitely, she
plucked up courage to ask, 'What did happen
between you and Marie-Claire?'

'We became engaged for the wrong reason.'

'Is that it?' she mocked bitterly, searching his
shuttered dark face. 'That's the sum total of your
ability to open up under questioning? Zero marks
out of ten, Christian!'

'*Bon, d'accord*!' he said tersely. 'I will tell you
my version, but you will not like what you hear.
Our families were friends. Pressure was put on
us both to marry. Marie-Claire was very keen to
marry the Malraux wealth, but unfortunately she
was in love with someone else, someone who did
not have any money...'

When he paused, with a sardonic glance at her,
she leaned forward. She felt so hungry for information, anything to throw light on Christian's
tortuous-sounding past, she could have shaken
him. 'Go on.'

'Do I need to? I regret my ego couldn't handle the idea of my intended wife preferring another man. When I discovered them together, and the truth was out, I broke off the engagement...'

'But...I thought Marie-Claire tried to commit suicide?' Emily stared at him uncomprehendingly. 'If she didn't even love you, then...'

'Her real lover dumped her also. Perhaps he'd been keen on the source of income, retaining a liaison with a rich man's wife?'

The cynical twist to the hard mouth was painful to witness. Emily shook her head slowly, trying to assimilate what he'd told her. 'But if that is what happened, why were you the villain of the piece, Christian? You'd committed no great sin, surely? Why the blame?'

He shrugged. He'd just peeled another *langoustine*, and he leaned forward and placed it between her parted lips, his face expressionless. She took a bite and then removed it quickly, annoyed with him, flushing slightly, unnerved by the casual, mocking intimacy.

'Everybody needs a scapegoat,' Christian was saying flatly. 'Besides, Marie-Claire begged me not to break our engagement. She vowed she loved me, and that she'd never see this other man again. I was too arrogant to relent. I didn't believe her. Deep down, I suspect I was glad of the excuse to be free. I probably wasn't ready for marriage, after all. Admitting that to myself doesn't make me feel any less guilty! And then, this was a quick-fire Greek tragedy. After the car crash, nobody was thinking clearly...'

'So Marie-Claire hated you for discovering her secret, and ruining her chances of being your wife? Mathieu was disillusioned with his hero, held you responsible for his beloved sister's suicide attempt, and came for a show-down?' Emily spoke with soft urgency, 'What happened then, Christian?'

Christian leaned back in his chair and took a hefty drink of wine. His gaze was disconcertingly steady as he considered the question.

'What happened then was one very emotional fifteen-year-old boy paying me a visit that same night, knocking back half a bottle of Château de Mordin *pineau cognac*, calling me all the names under the sun, accusing me of mental cruelty, and continuing his verbal abuse as I drove him home,' Christian said quietly.

His eyes were slits of blue against the sun, his face darkening in memory. 'And then we crashed, head-on, into a tree... And that young boy never walked again. This...' he briefly touched the scar on his cheek, livid white in the deep tan of his skin '...was all I had to show for it. So yes, I felt guilty. I felt responsible...! I walked free, leaving other people's lives wrecked around me! Wouldn't *you* feel guilty and responsible, Emily?'

'But, Christian, it was an accident...!'

'Nothing in this life is an accident, Emily.' The flicker of gaunt self-reproach in his eyes seemed to twist her stomach in knots. 'I might have had

a few mitigating circumstances, but through my
own actions, through my pride, my arrogance
over Marie-Claire, I'd brought about the whole
tragic sequence. Who *wouldn't* feel guilty
and responsible?'

CHAPTER NINE

THE *grand bal* was in full swing.

The floodlit grounds of the château were
thronging with people. Voices and laughter
drifted on the warm, scented night air. In the distance, the local band, '*Alain Lenoir et son
Orchestre*' as they were billed importantly around
the village, were pounding out an imaginative
version of an old Beatles song, sung in English
in wonderfully Gallic accents. Fairy-lights
twinkled around the creeper-clad courtyard,
where the dancing was going on. The château was
unrecognisable. Emily couldn't remember feeling
so utterly, bleakly despairing, in such a breath-
takingly beautiful setting...

'Come and dance with me, Emily.'

From her hiding place by the old cedar tree on
the lawn Emily spun round abruptly at the sound
of Christian's voice. His wry, softly menacing
tone was totally at odds with the lightness of the
words. He towered tall and dark behind her, devastatingly attractive in formal white dinner-
jacket and dark trousers. She felt the breath leave
her body in a rush.

'I'm not really in the mood for dancing...'

'But I am. I'm also in the mood for hearing
an explanation of just where the *hell* you dis-

appeared to last night, and most of today?' he enquired grimly. He was spectacularly angry, she realised, with a sinking stomach. She'd had a feeling he might be . . .

Stiff and tense in her pale peach silk dress, the prettiest, most morale-boosting outfit she'd been able to find on her shopping trip earlier this morning, she stared up at him.

'I rang. Didn't Lisette give you my message?' she countered calmly.

'It was a rather *cryptic* message.'

'I went into Saintes.' She felt him tense warily, and a fresh wave of apprehension rippled silently through her.

'You went to see your friends, the Colberts.'

She met his eyes with a slight nod, blinking involuntarily at the furious brilliance of his gaze.

'I had a feeling that's where you'd gone.'

'Quite. Now you know. And you don't have to be polite and ask me to dance,' she pointed out with soft sarcasm. 'It's so out of character . . .'

'Come here . . .' Leaving her no choice, he took her hand and pulled her firmly up the sloping lawn to the courtyard. She found herself fighting for poise and struggling to combat the heat of his body as he held her close. Moving against him on the crowded dance floor had a disturbing effect. Caught in his arms, forced to dance the classic French 'slow', was not the way she'd have chosen to spend her last night at Château de Mordin. And she'd already braced herself mentally to leave tomorrow . . .

The anger seethed beneath the surface. 'Sorry, did you want me for something last night?' It was deliberately cool and provocative. The narrow, hostile gaze darkened beneath furrowed black brows.

'It would have been good manners to let me know you were going!' He was suppressing his temper with visible difficulty. 'Instead of just disappearing!'

'Good manners? I'm so sorry,' she said sweetly. 'I thought you might try to stop me.'

He expelled his breath angrily. 'Why in God's name would I have wanted to stop you?'

'Stupid of me. Of course you wouldn't. You'd have been glad of the break!' She glared defiantly over his shoulder, willing herself to stay calm, to fail to respond to the ruthless pressure of his hands on her back. The halter-dress was backless, and swirled in soft peach silk to mid-calf. As his lean fingers smoothed the bare warmth of her skin from waist to armpits she found herself fervently wishing she'd chosen something more matronly for her last night as Christian Malraux's secretary...

'I just had to get away, that's all...' After yesterday's outing she'd been too panic-stricken by the intensity of her feelings to face spending any more time in Christian's company.

Despite the lighter episode of the wind-surfing, the relaxation of the sun and sand, they'd driven back from the coast with nothing resolved. If anything, their brief spell of rapport, the joking and banter over the wind-surfing, the pleasure of the picnic, had made her feel the rift between them more deeply.

Christian's confidences about events of five years back seemed to have moved them no closer together. As far as Emily could judge, through her haze of blind misery, neither had it brought them any closer to 'parting as friends'.

Back at the château she'd been consumed with the need to escape. She'd jumped in her Renault, made an emergency call to Marianne from the telephone in the village, and headed for her friend's flat in Saintes...

With good reason, judging by his mood tonight. What a selfish, arrogant *bastard* he was! He felt guilty, he was sorry he'd allowed it to start, he wanted to end their steamy little liaison, but on *his* terms, under *his* control! If she took matters into her own hands, just disappeared for the night without asking permission, he flew into another of his black rages...

And she had to end it. She couldn't take any more emotional punishment. She had to get out. The only reason she'd come back tonight was a perverse desire to see Christian reconciled with the Colberts. Because they *would* come. After seeing them all last night, she was more or less sure of it...

'I stayed with Marianne,' she told him briefly, avoiding his eyes. 'We went round to her parents' house, so I saw Mathieu, too. And his fiancée. She seems really nice...'

Christian seemed to have his anger under control now.

'I'm glad. Glad that Mathieu has someone.' His deep voice was curt. 'Emily, last night, I wanted to——'

'In fact, he's pretty mobile now,' she cut in quickly, bracing herself for defence. If Christian started on his 'parting as friends' tack again, she knew she'd crack, burst into humiliating tears, make an utter fool of herself... 'He can get around very efficiently in an electronic wheelchair. You remember how artistic he always was? He has a job in a pottery, helping to glaze and decorate the pots. It was so nice to see him again. It's hard to believe he's twenty! Last time I saw him he was only fourteen...'

'Emily, will you shut up?' Christian growled at her softly, ducking his head to catch her unawares, silencing her babble of talk with his mouth. The hard, demanding thrust of his tongue inside the warmth of her mouth made her involuntarily close her eyes, convulsively slide her fingers along his shoulders, lace them around his neck.

She was lost in the bitter pain of the embrace, powerless to curb the intense heat of longing he could arouse in her. A shudder went through his body as he drew her closer. He held her so close that she could almost imagine he might never let her go...

'Christian? Excuse me?' Lisette's voice cut in on them. Emily jerked free, turning to see the

French girl smiling coolly, regarding Emily's flushed appearance and Christian's dark scowl with admirable composure. 'There is someone looking for you.'

'*Merci*, Lisette,' There was a wealth of wry mockery in Christian's response. He kept his arm possessively around Emily's shoulders. 'I hope it is someone *very* important?'

Lisette, sexy and curvaceous in clinging black, gave him a reproachful look before she turned and waved her arm across the dance-floor. Mathieu Colbert sat there, in his wheelchair. His fiancée, Jeanne, a pretty girl in a flowery sun-dress, stood beside him.

Christian tensed, his arm rigid on Emily's shoulders. Releasing her abruptly, he dropped his head to search her blank face.

'Is this your doing?' he queried, with soft fury.

'Go and talk to Mathieu.'

The look he gave her, as he began to slowly push through the crowd, was disbelieving, wry with self-mockery.

'If it's a lynching party, you've only yourself to blame!'

'Don't be such a pessimist. Time is a great healer,' she heard herself saying idiotically. She was rewarded by an oblique glance, reminiscent of an adult humouring a vexatious child.

Alone in the swirl of dancers, she watched the scene from a distance, like a tableau without words. Christian, tall, dark, braced as if for battle, hands thrust into the pockets of his dark evening trousers, and Mathieu, pale and blond-haired, with a dreamy, artistic air about him. They faced each other for what looked to be an endless silence. Then Mathieu slowly held out his hand, and Christian moved at last, bent to clasp the outstretched hand, then embraced the younger man in a fierce Gallic style which brought a lump to Emily's throat.

The three of them, Mathieu, Jeanne and Christian, turned together and began to make their way towards the château, out of sight.

Emerging from her preoccupation, Emily realised she was standing alone, like an idiot, in the centre of dancing couples. She slowly made her way off the dance-floor, her heart twisting with an odd kind of happiness at the thought of Christian finally confronting the ghosts of the past, finally getting the chance to talk things out with Mathieu. If nothing else came of their brief relationship, she told herself, this was something good. Something good had come of it...

Lisette was hovering on the edge of the dancers.

'Wait.' She caught at Emily's arm. 'I want to talk to you.'

'Yes?'

Emily eyed the French girl warily. The animosity between them had never faded. She wasn't altogether surprised when Lisette went on in a small, contemptuous voice, 'You are making a fool of yourself with Christian. Do you realise that?'

'Lisette, I really don't want to discuss Christian with you...'

'No? More fool you! You might learn something! He is not interested in your stupid little English *crush*! He's not interested in your pathetic, *bourgeoise* values and your boring, inept lovemaking...'

'Lisette, be quiet...' The other girl's hatred made Emily feel quite sick.

'He told me! Don't you know he is laughing about you, behind your back? I see in your room that you have already packed your suitcase. So why don't you go back to England now, leave tonight, before the whole village enjoys the joke?'

The cool green stare moved over Emily's slender figure in the peach silk dress, taking in the freshly washed blonde curls feathered softly round her high-cheekboned face, the telltale flicker of uncertainty in the wide, vulnerable brown eyes.

'Do you want to be the village joke?' Lisette persisted, softly venomous.

'Perhaps the joke is on you?' Emily countered quietly, making a huge effort to strike back. 'Perhaps you should confine your childish abuse to your conversations with Greg Vernon? Look, he's over there. Frankly he's the only person I can think of who would appreciate this kind of thing...'

Flicking her arm free of the girl's grasp, she walked quickly away, head held high. Up in her room, though, pride dissolved into panic and despair. Lisette might be stirring up trouble, but in essence she was right. Didn't her unkind, vicious words echo some of Christian's own sentiments? Like his opinion that there were girls good for sensational sex, and girls good for marrying and settling down?

Almost without conscious volition she found herself collecting her remaining possessions, throwing them into bags with trembling urgency.

Dashing away hot tears of humiliation, Emily tore a row of clothes from the wardrobe, and hurled them uncaringly into her suitcase.

So much for not being the 'running-away' type. Enough was enough. She wasn't made of stone. She might be awarding Lisette an undeserved victory by going now, as suggested. But she was past caring. She couldn't take any more. Being embroiled in this hothouse of passion and jealousy and uncertainty was more than she felt mentally or emotionally able to cope with...

It was pure luck that no one saw her throwing her luggage into the car. She was too upset for it to matter either way. White-faced and trembling, she steered the Renault as fast as she dared down the château's long gravelled drive. The powerful lights of the car behind her dazzled in her mirror as she approached the grey stone gates. But it wasn't until it roared past her, on the grass, then swerved aggressively across to block her exit, forcing her to stop, that she realised it was Christian's Mercedes.

Her heart plummeted crazily in her chest. She watched him jump out of his car and stride rapidly towards her, the white dinner-jacket flapping loose, dazzling in the headlights. In blind fury she put the heel of her hand on the horn and left it there. The raucous blare shattered the peace of the evening.

'Well, well, if it isn't Mademoiselle Gainsborough, doing another moonlight flit!' he murmured drily, leaning on her open window, and wrenching her hand off the horn with a decisive movement. Arm-wrestling ferociously against his strength, she was easily defeated. In the abrupt contrast of silence, only her rapid, shallow breathing could be heard. He directed a searching, penetrating gaze into her shadowed face.

'Fortunately, Emily, I caught you this time...'

'I am *not* doing a moonlight flit,' she spat, with shaky anger. 'I'm going back to England. I haven't stolen any money. The château's silver is untouched. So if you don't move your car I'll drive into it...!'

Muttering a short, lamentably coarse oath, Christian ripped open the door and hauled her forcefully out of the car.

'You're not going anywhere!' he grated. 'You're coming back to the château with me...'

'*No*! Let go of me! I'm warning you, Christian...'

'You're *warning* me? Why don't you just stop struggling and admit when you're beaten?'

At his arrogant words, a dark haze of anger engulfed her. Every detail of her judo training raced to her rescue. With reflexes born of hysteria and fury she grabbed his forearm, braced, flexed, twisted, and although Christian failed to fly satisfyingly into the air he was nevertheless abruptly flipped off balance. To her secret astonishment he fell, landing with a heavy, sickening thud on the grass verge beside the car. He lay still. He looked unconscious.

Stunned, breathing rapidly, she stared down at him. He wasn't moving. She couldn't even see him breathing...

Fear rushed at her so unexpectedly that she felt almost faint. She felt glued to the spot, her eyes fixed on his dark face, the inert length of his body.

'Christian? *Christian*...?' Beside herself now, stifling sobs of fear and anguish, she dropped to her knees. Had he hit his head on a stone? Caught it on the bumper of the car, maybe, as he fell? Emily chewed her lip distractedly, wildly disjointed thoughts scattering through her head. She was shivering. She felt cold, cold and trembling with a terrible, gut-wrenching fear. What had she *done* to him? If he was really hurt, she'd never forgive herself...

Despite the festive sounds drifting in the night air from the *grand bal*, there wasn't a soul nearby. Presumably the entire village was up in the château's courtyard, awaiting the promised midnight firework display. The wind rustled in the trees, and black shapes rapidly flitted and darted overhead. The bats again. Were they some kind of omen for her?

Shuddering, she slid her hands over the muscular warmth of Christian's chest, inside his silk-lined jacket, felt the ridges of his pectoral muscles, the scratch of coarse chest-hair under the fine silk of his shirt. Locating his heart in the darkness, she felt the heart-beat thudding steady and strong. Slightly reassured, she bent closer, inhaled the familiar intoxicating smell of his subtle, expensive after-shave, sandalwood and musk.

'Christian, please . . . oh, *please* wake up . . . !'

She was tentatively touching his dark face, running her fingers along the abrasive trace of stubble on his hard jawline, when without warning his hand snaked up to capture her.

With a yelp of shocked surprise she found herself dragged down so that she tumbled beside him on the grass, then pinned there, with a swiftness which betrayed a suspicious lack of injury. Flattened on the cool, scratchy grass, she glared up at his wickedly mocking smile in furious resentment.

'You were play-acting?' she demanded chokingly. 'How *could* you do that? I was worried sick, thought I'd *killed* you, you hateful beast . . .'

'Nice to know you care. It would take a lot more than your enchanting judo techniques to kill me off, Emily.'

'Let me up!' She kicked and bucked beneath him, but she couldn't move.

'Not until you promise to behave yourself. Not until you promise to come back quietly, like a good girl, to the château...'

'Why? Just so you can have a bit more fun at my expense? Why can't you just leave me alone?' Tears of anger and frustration and humiliation were trickling down her temples, wetting her hair. She gulped them back, hating herself for such despicable weakness.

'It's impossible,' he told her huskily, taking her wet face in his hands and gazing steadily into her eyes.

'What's impossible?' It was an angry whisper as she writhed once more to free herself, succeeding only in bringing their bodies into closer, more agonising contact.

He increased the weight of his body to imprison her beneath him, grasping her wrists above her head, pinning her legs still with his own. Abruptly, the battle was over. She felt the fight go out of her.

'It is impossible for me to leave you alone, Emily. And what *fun* have I had at your expense?'

'Watching the naïve little English girl with the giant crush on you?' she choked bitterly. 'Don't tell me you haven't enjoyed the joke! Can't you see it's better if I go now? I just want to go back to England, and your life can get...uncomplicated again...'

'I don't want my life uncomplicated again,' he mocked gently, moving to release her, beginning to haul her to her feet, 'If uncomplicated is how my life was before you came along, Emily, I like it complicated.'

'Christian...' She stopped, dimly registering what he'd said.

'I'm sick of talking in riddles. I don't understand,' she began in a choked, angry voice. He steadied them both upright, then pulled her into his arms.

'I am not sure that I understand, either,' he agreed quietly. There was no trace of mockery or taunting now. Only an intent regard, steady as he gazed at her, his eyes unnervingly brilliant as he searched her face. 'All I know for sure, Emily, is that I cannot let you go!'

'Isn't kidnapping illegal in France?'

'Probably.' His smile was a wry twist. He raked her appearance from head to toe. 'Were you planning on catching a plane in your evening dress, Emily?'

She glanced down. In her blind haste to escape after Lisette's venomous attack, she'd forgotten to change out of her peach silk dress.

'I was in a hurry.' The rather weak explanation was smothered as he crushed her close to his chest, with a rough, choked laugh.

His mouth was warm and possessive as he bent to kiss her. Lifting her face warily, still unsure precisely where this was all leading, she parted her lips to the hungry invasion.

'Sweet, adorable little Emily...' He mouthed the words with husky emphasis as he trailed small, intense kisses along her jawline, down the soft curve of her neck, over the fragile swell of her earlobe. 'Have you truly no idea how much I love you?'

She went very still in his arms. Her heart was beating faster than the bats' wings high above them. Searching his dark face incredulously, she shook her head.

'I have truly no idea at all,' she agreed unsteadily, her throat tightening. 'Christian, don't say this...if it's not true, I couldn't bear it...'

'*Quelle espèce d'idiot*!' he muttered softly, tightening his hold on her again until she was forced to encircle him totally with her arms, to cling so close she felt his heat warm right through to her heart. 'You little idiot! You think I would say such a thing and not mean it? Emily *ma mignonne*...I love you. *Je t'aime. Je t'aime beaucoup! C'est vrai!* Believe me, *ma petite*. It is true!'

She blinked up at him, tears blurring her vision.

'It is?' she ventured shakily. She was half laughing, half crying. And shaking, shaking all over, so badly she was afraid she'd fall over. 'Oh, Christian, hold me...please...?'

'I am holding you, Emily,' he murmured, with wry, husky tenderness.

'I'm sorry to be so ridiculously...emotional,' she went on faintly. 'It's just that... I love you too! And I thought you didn't love me...'

'*Et voilà*!' He bent his head to smile at her, the victorious slash of white in his dark face reminding her of his monumental arrogance. Tensing slightly, she made a half-hearted attempt to push him away.

'You needn't look so smug!' she whispered, smiling back so radiantly he raggedly caught his breath. 'And you might at least have the chivalry to look a little...surprised?'

He gave her a slight, impatient shake. 'Don't start fighting me again, Emily. I hoped... I had some notion that perhaps you cared for me a little...'

'Liar! You've been basking in the warmth of my girlish infatuation ever since I came here.'

His dark face had become serious as he returned her stare. 'No. You're wrong. I have been sweating like a condemned man, wondering if you were real, if you would ever stay with me, wondering if my luck might truly hold, long enough for me to make this last...'

'Oh, Christian...' It was no use. She dissolved into helpless, utterly reprehensible tears. Laughing softly, he held her face against his chest while she soaked the smooth silk of his shirt. The emotion she felt threatened to overwhelm her. She clung to him in mindless happiness, too stunned by it all to think straight.

They stood like that for a long time, locked together. Finally, Christian gently disengaged them and, gripping a protective arm round her shoulders, steered her towards the Mercedes. Feeling too weak-kneed to move, she meekly agreed to sit in the passenger seat while Christian rapidly manoeuvred the Renault on to the grass and locked it up, then returned to drive them back up to the château.

In the lamplit privacy of his apartment, with the curtains drawn against the revellers in the courtyard below, they stared at each other in vague disbelief.

'You've got grass stains on your white DJ,' she pointed out softly, biting her lip as he proceeded to shrug it off and toss it into the corner of the room.

'I'll make sure you get the cleaning bill,' he teased.

He'd begun tugging unsteadily at his bow-tie, and then stopped with it half-undone, hesitating, shooting a hot, impatient glance towards her before striding over to the drinks cupboard and pouring them both a stiff brandy.

A smile tugged irresistibly at the corners of her mouth as she watched his uncharacteristic self-control. She could almost read his mind. The wave of love she felt was almost a physical spasm somewhere around her solar plexus. She'd never realised she could be so deeply emotional.

'*Dieu*, Emily. Don't look at me like that! If I haul you off to bed right now, your suspicions

will be confirmed. That sex is my only interest...'
His grin was rueful, the dark gleam in his eyes
leaving her in no doubt of his intentions later.

'Isn't it?' she queried innocently. 'I thought
that was what you were trying to tell me, at your
beach house?'

The blue eyes darkened. He raked a jerky
finger round the collar of his evening shirt,
flipping open the top button.

'No. That is not what I was trying to tell you,
Emily. If you had listened, I said that sexual attraction has never before involved so many emotions for me.'

His soft, husky tone held a fine thread of steel
beneath the velvet. She blinked at the humorous
intensity of his gaze. Her eyes felt magnetically
held in his. She could feel her throat tightening
in response.

There was a charged pause. He loosened his
shoulders in a shrug, and said, 'So tell me, what
made you rush off in that blind fury tonight?'

The question was aimed with such careless
precision that she was taken by surprise.

'I...it was a combination of things...'

'It wouldn't have been something Lisette said,
by any chance?'

'Partly... But I'd already decided to go,
Christian. Yesterday you were virtually telling me
it was all over! Lisette just...hastened the
decision...'

'I know Lisette has been stirring up trouble.
She will be leaving.' The deep voice was coolly

decisive. 'Now that I have decided to stay, she will go. If she behaves herself until she leaves, she'll get a good reference. She'll have no trouble finding another similar job.'

Emily nodded slowly. In spite of everything, she found herself feeling a faint *frisson* of sympathy for the other girl.

'And you're wrong. About what I was saying yesterday...'

Christian raked a shaky hand through his dark hair, expelling his breath heavily as he met her uncertain gaze. 'I wasn't sure where I stood! You made it clear you felt something for me. But when I feared Marianne would have well and truly crucified my reputation, and then I saw you in the café with that...oaf, Vernon...'

'And I saw Lisette slinking out of your rooms?' she intercepted softly.

'As God is my witness, Emily, nothing happened...'

'I believe you!'

'But you wouldn't come to Paris with me.'

'Because I knew I'd fallen in love with you. I couldn't face getting in any deeper, not when I thought there was no chance for us...'

'But whenever I tried to talk about how I felt, you switched the subject, faster than the speed of light...!'

'You told me love was a destructive emotion.'

'I was wrong.'

'Yes...'

There was another short, charged silence. Taking a gulp of his brandy, Christian said quietly, 'So do you want to know what Mathieu had to say? Or do you already know? Did he tell you last night?'

She shook her head, taking the brandy glass he proferred with a shaky smile.

'He didn't tell me last night. But I knew he'd come. I'd been hoping he would ever since Marianne told me how upset he was when he heard you'd come back. I guessed he'd have as much need to talk things through as you did...'

'He'd been feeling guilty too,' Christian summed up thoughtfully, coming to sit close to her on the kilim-draped sofa. Shivers of pleasure raced along her bare shoulders as he rested his arm behind her. 'He'd suppressed all the memories of the crash. It wasn't until I came back and stirred up all this fresh hatred and hostility in his family that he remembered grabbing the steering-wheel that night...'

She stared at him in silence. Christian's eyes were brilliantly blue as he stared back at her.

'I see! So *that's* what happened.'

'Yes. It is.'

'But...surely, you knew that all along? *You* hadn't forgotten?'

He shook his head slowly, his expression unreadable. 'What difference did it make? Mathieu was still disabled for life. Pointing the finger at him didn't change anything...'

'But you took all the...slander! Marianne even thought you were drunk!'

'It was young Mathieu who was drunk,' Christian said quietly. 'But, in essence, the whole damned tragedy was still my fault...'

'*Don't*!' She clicked her glass down on the table and took Christian's from his hand, depositing it in the same place. With a militant glitter in her brown eyes she grasped his shoulders, and gave him a warning shake. 'Don't start that guilt trip again!'

He shook his head, laughter in his eyes as he slid his hands round her slender ribcage, caressed the sides of her breasts with his thumbs.

'It's all right, Emily. With my little "guardian angel" to supervise, guilt trips are a thing of the past...'

'Are you sure? You mean that?'

'I mean it. Will you marry me?'

Taken aback at the abruptness of the proposal, she swallowed, gazing at him in shock. '*Marry* you?' she echoed stupidly.

'Marry me. That is, become my wife,' he explained patiently, the deep voice thickening with amused emotion as the colour surged and receded in her face. 'Forsake all others, *ma petite*? Wear my ring? Become Madame Malraux?'

She damped down the idiotic dance of joy in her heart. Pretending to consider it solemnly, she fixed him with a grave, wide-eyed stare.

'Abandon my Foreign Office career?' She frowned pensively. 'Just to become your sex slave, Monsieur Malraux?'

With a growl of anguish, he caught her to him, crushing the breath out of her, 'Emily, don't torture me, *ma mignonne*. Pursue whatever career you want. Run for Prime Minister if you wish. But please, *je t'en prie, chérie*, I beg you, stay with me?'

'Well, I suppose I could consider reforming an "original sinner" as an *alternative* career...'

Christian's harsh face had paled with tension. Emotion flamed in his darkened eyes. The dimple in her cheek betrayed her as she laughed up at his grim expression, shivering deliciously as she wrapped herself more closely around him, felt a shudder go through him, felt the heat kindling out of control between them.

'*Emily* ...!'

'All right,' she whispered breathlessly, sliding her fingers into his hair and seeking his hard mouth with a trail of soft, loving kisses along his jawbone. 'I accept. But you'll have to remind me of the major perks of the job...'

'Shameless!' he grated thickly against her hair, standing up and hauling her with him. His eyes were brilliant with triumph as he gazed down at her flushed, laughing face. 'Irrepressible...'

He twisted her firmly round, unfastened the halter-neck of her dress. 'What is more, this dress will have to come off. There are grass stains all over it, *ma mignonne*...'

'I'll be sure to send you the cleaning bill!'

As the peach silk slithered to her waist there was a distant volley of fireworks beyond the heavy kilim curtains, a dazzled sigh of approval from the crowd.

'This feels like stripping off for an invisible audience!' Emily laughed breathlessly, spinning round and wrapping herself around him so tightly that he was forced to lift her up into his arms, and carry her towards the bedroom.

'With you as the star of the show, *ma petite...*'

'I want you to make love to me now,' she whispered unsteadily. 'Right now, Christian...!'

There was the sound of more fireworks, another collective cheer from the crowded courtyard below, then a rapturous round of applause. Their eyes met, and they both started to laugh.

'At least somebody approves, even if you've yet to make an honest woman of me,' she murmured, smiling up at him incandescently.

'Sinful...' he growled softly, laying her on the bed. His smile was devastating as he surveyed his prize.

'Blissful,' she corrected, with a faint blush colouring her cheeks, tugging him down to her. 'Loving someone the way I love you, Christian, could never, ever be a sin!'

Take 4 bestselling love stories FREE

Plus get a FREE surprise gift!

HARLEQUIN®

Deceit, betrayal, murder

Join Harlequin's intrepid heroines, India Leigh
and Mary Hadfield, as they ferret out the truth
behind the mysterious goings-on in their
neighborhood. These two women are no milk-
and-water misses. In fact, they thrive on

MISCHIEF & MAYHEM

Watch for their incredible adventures in this
special two-book collection. Available in March,
wherever Harlequin books are sold.

HARLEQUIN®

PRESENTS Plus

Lindsey and Tim Ramsden were married—but, these
days, in name only. Their once-passionate relationship
hadn't survived a bitter misunderstanding, and they were
separated by time and the Atlantic Ocean. Now Lindsey
had another chance at happiness; could she accept that
her marriage was finally over, and that it was time to
move on?

*"The first man to walk through this door will be the one I
date for a month...."* And he turned out to be Leo
Kozakis—the man who had cruelly rejected Jacy ten
years before! The sensible thing would be to forget the
wager, but Jacy was seized by another reckless impulse:
she was more than a match now for Leo—and she would
seize her chances for passion...and revenge!

Presents Plus is Passion Plus!

Coming next month:

The Wrong Kind of Wife by Roberta Leigh
Harlequin Presents Plus #1725

and

Gamble on Passion by Jacqueline Baird
Harlequin Presents Plus #1726

Harlequin Presents Plus
The best has just gotten better!

Available in March wherever Harlequin books are sold.

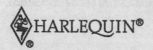

HARLEQUIN®

Don't miss these Harlequin favorites by some of our most distinguished authors!
And now, you can receive a discount by ordering two or more titles!

HT#25577	WILD LIKE THE WIND by Janice Kaiser	$2.99	☐
HT#25589	THE RETURN OF CAINE O'HALLORAN by JoAnn Ross	$2.99	☐
HP#11626	THE SEDUCTION STAKES by Lindsay Armstrong	$2.99	☐
HP#11647	GIVE A MAN A BAD NAME by Roberta Leigh	$2.99	☐
HR#03293	THE MAN WHO CAME FOR CHRISTMAS by Bethany Campbell	$2.89	☐
HR#03308	RELATIVE VALUES by Jessica Steele	$2.89	☐
SR#70589	CANDY KISSES by Muriel Jensen	$3.50	☐
SR#70598	WEDDING INVITATION by Marisa Carroll	$3.50 U.S. $3.99 CAN.	☐
HI#22230	CACHE POOR by Margaret St. George	$2.99	☐
HAR#16515	NO ROOM AT THE INN by Linda Randall Wisdom	$3.50	☐
HAR#16520	THE ADVENTURESS by M.J. Rodgers	$3.50	☐
HS#28795	PIECES OF SKY by Marianne Willman	$3.99	☐
HS#28824	A WARRIOR'S WAY by Margaret Moore	$3.99 U.S. $4.50 CAN.	☐

(limited quantities available on certain titles)

	AMOUNT	$
DEDUCT:	**10% DISCOUNT FOR 2+ BOOKS**	$
ADD:	**POSTAGE & HANDLING**	$
	($1.00 for one book, 50¢ for each additional)	
	APPLICABLE TAXES*	$_____
	TOTAL PAYABLE	$_____
	(check or money order—please do not send cash)	

To order, complete this form and send it, along with a check or money order for the total above, payable to Harlequin Books, to: **In the U.S.:** 3010 Walden Avenue, P.O. Box 9047, Buffalo, NY 14269-9047; **In Canada:** P.O. Box 613, Fort Erie, Ontario, L2A 5X3.

Name:_____

Address:_____ City:_____

State/Prov.:_____ Zip/Postal Code:_____

*New York residents remit applicable sales taxes.
Canadian residents remit applicable GST and provincial taxes.

HBACK-JM2